Francis Hopkinson Smith, Bruce Rogers

The Other Fellow

Francis Hopkinson Smith, Bruce Rogers

The Other Fellow

ISBN/EAN: 9783743367029

Manufactured in Europe, USA, Canada, Australia, Japa

Cover: Foto ©Andreas Hilbeck / pixelio.de

Manufactured and distributed by brebook publishing software (www.brebook.com)

Francis Hopkinson Smith, Bruce Rogers

The Other Fellow

The Other Fellow

By F. HOPKINSON SMITH

BOSTON AND NEW YORK
HOUGHTON, MIFFLIN AND COMPANY
The Riverside Press, Cambridge
1899

CONTENTS

LIST OF ILLUSTRATIONS

DICK SANDS, CONVICT. I

THE stage stopped at a disheartened-looking tavern with a sagging porch and sprawling wooden steps. A fat man with a good-natured face, tagged with a gray chin whisker, bareheaded, and without a coat — there was snow on the ground, too — and who said he was the landlord, lifted my yellow bag from one of the long chintz-covered stage cushions, and preceded me through a sanded hall into a low-ceiled room warmed by a red-hot stove, and lighted by windows filled with geraniums in full bloom. The effect of this color was so surprising, and the contrast to the desolate surroundings outside so grateful, that, without stopping to register my name, I drew up a chair and joined the circle of baking loungers. My oversight was promptly noted by the clerk — a sallow-faced young man with an uncomfortably high collar, red necktie, and stooping shoulders — and as promptly corrected by his dipping a pen in a wooden inkstand and holding the book on his knee until I could add my own superscription to those on its bespattered page. He had been considerate enough not to ask me to rise.

The landlord studied the signature, his spectacles on his nose, and remarked in a kindly tone:—

"Oh, you're the man what's going to lecture to the college."

"Yes; how far is it from here?"

"'Bout two miles out, Bingville way. You'll want a team, won't you? If I'd knowed it was you when yer got out I'd told the driver to come back for you. But it's all right—he's got to stop here again in half an hour—soon's he leaves the mail."

I thanked him and asked him to see that the stage called for me at half-past seven, as I was to speak at eight o'clock. He nodded in assent, dropped into a rocking chair, and guided a spittoon into range with his foot. Then he backed away a little and began to scrutinize my face. Something about me evidently puzzled him. A leaning mirror that hung over a washstand reflected his head and shoulders, and gave me every expression that flitted across his good-natured countenance.

His summing up was evidently favorable, for his scrutinizing look gave place to a benign smile which widened into curves around his mouth and lost itself in faint ripples under his eyes. Hitching his chair closer, he spread his fat knees, and settled his broad shoulders, lazily stroking his chin whisker all the while with his puffy fingers.

"Guess you ain't been at the business long," he said kindly. "Last one we had a year ago looked kinder peaked." The secret of his peculiar interest was now out. "Must be awful tough on yer throat, havin' to holler so. I was n't up to the show, but the fellers said they heard him 'fore they got to the crossin'. 'T was spring weather and the winders was up. He did n't have no baggage — only a paper box and a strap. I got supper for him when he come back, and he did eat hearty — did me good to watch him." Then, looking at the clock and recalling his duties as a host, he leaned over, and shielding his mouth with his hand, so as not to be overheard by the loungers, said in a confidential tone, "Supper 'll be on in half an hour, if you want to clean up. I 'll see you get what you want. Your room 's first on the right — you can't miss it."

I expressed my appreciation of his timely suggestion, and picking up the yellow bag myself — hall-boys are scarce in these localities — mounted the steps to my bedroom.

Within the hour — fully equipped in the regulation costume, swallow-tail, white tie, and white waistcoat — I was again hugging the stove, for my bedroom had been as cold as a barn.

My appearance created something of a sensation. A tall man in a butternut suit, with a sinister face, craned his head as I passed, and the sallow-faced clerk leaned over the desk in an absorbed way, his eyes glued to my shirt front. The others looked stolidly at the red bulb of the stove. No remarks were made — none aloud, the splendor of my appearance and the immaculate nature of my appointments seeming to have paralyzed general conversation for the moment. This silence continued. I confess I did not know how to break it. Tavern stoves are often trying ordeals to the wayfarer; the silent listeners with the impassive leather faces and foxlike eyes disconcert him; he knows just what they will say about him when they go out. The awkward stillness was finally broken by a girl in blue gingham opening a door and announcing supper.

It was one of those frying-pan feasts of eggs, bacon, and doughnuts, with canned corn in birds' bathtubs, plenty of green pickles, and dabs of home-made preserves in pressed glass saucers. It occupied a few moments only. When it was over, I resumed my chair by the stove.

The night had evidently grown colder. The landlord had felt it, for he had put on his coat; so had a man with a dyed mustache and heavy red face, whom I had left tipped back against the wall, and who was now raking out the ashes with a poker. So had the butternut man, who had moved two diameters nearer the centre of comfort. All doubts, however, were dispelled by the arrival of a thickset man with ruddy cheeks, who slammed the door behind him and moved quickly toward the stove, shedding the snow from his high boots as he walked. He nodded to the landlord and spread his stiff fingers to the red glow. A faint wreath of white steam arose from his coonskin overcoat, filling the room with the odor of wet horse blankets and burned leather. The landlord left the desk, where he had been figuring with the clerk, approached my chair, and pointing to the new arrival, said: —

"This is the driver I been expectin' over from Hell's Diggings. He 'll take you. This man" — he now pointed to me — "wants to go to the college at 7.30."

The new arrival shifted his whip to the other hand, looked me all over, his keen and penetrating eye resting for an instant on my white shirt and waistcoat, and answered slowly, still looking at me, but addressing the landlord : —

" He 'll have to get somebody else. I got to take Dick Sands over to Millwood Station ; his mother 's took bad again."

" What, Dick Sands ? " came a voice from the other side of the stove. It was the man in the butternut suit.

"Why, Dick Sands," replied the driver in a positive tone.

" Not *Dick Sands ?* " The voice expressed not only surprise but incredulity.

" Yes, DICK SANDS," shouted the driver in a tone that carried with it his instant intention of breaking anybody's head who doubted the statement.

" Gosh ! that so ? When did he git out ? " cried the butternut man.

" Oh, a month back. He 's been up in Hell's Diggin's ever since." Then finding that no one impugned his veracity, he added in a milder tone : " His old mother 's awful sick up to her sister's back of Millwood. He got word a while ago."

" Well, this gentleman 's got to speak at the college, and our team won't be back in time." The landlord pronounced the word " gentleman " with emphasis. The white waistcoat had evidently gotten in its fine work.

"Let Dick walk," broke in the clerk. "He 's used to it, and used to runnin', too" — this last with a dry laugh in spite of an angry glance from his employer.

"Well, Dick won't walk," snapped the driver, his voice rising. "He 'll ride like a white man, he will, and that 's all there is to it. His leg 's bad ag'in."

These remarks were not aimed at me nor at the room. They were fired pointblank at the clerk. I kept silent; so did the clerk.

"What time was you goin' to take Dick?" inquired the landlord in a conciliatory tone.

"'Bout 7.20 — time to catch the 8.10."

"Well, now, why can't you take this man along? You can go to the Diggings for Dick, and then" — pointing again at me — "you can drop him at the college and keep on to the station. 'T ain't much out of the way."

The driver scanned me closely and answered coldly: —

"Guess his kind don't want to mix in with Dick" — and started for the door.

"I have no objection," I answered meekly, "provided I can reach the lecture hall in time."

The driver halted, hit the spittoon squarely

in the middle, and said with deep earnestness and with a slight trace of deference :—

"Guess you don't know it all, stranger. Dick 's served time. Been up twice."

"Convict ?" — my voice evidently betrayed my surprise.

"You 've struck it fust time — last trip was for five years."

He stood whip in hand, his fur cap pulled over his ears, his eyes fixed on mine, noting the effect of the shot. Every other eye in the room was similarly occupied.

I had no desire to walk to Bingville in the cold. I felt, too, the necessity of proving myself up to the customary village standard in courage and complacency.

"That don't worry me a bit, my friend. There are a good many of us out of jail that ought to be in, and a good many in that ought to be out." I said this calmly, like a man of wide experience and knowledge of the world, one who had traveled extensively, and whose knowledge of convicts and other shady characters was consequently large and varied. The prehistoric age of this epigram was apparently unnoticed by the driver, for he started forward, grasped my hand, and blurted out in a whole-souled, hearty way, strangely in contrast with his former manner : —

"You ain't so gol-darned stuck up, be ye? Yes, I'll take ye, and glad to." Then he stooped over and laid his hand on my shoulder and said in a softened voice: "When ye git 'longside o' Dick you tell him that; it'll please him," and he stalked out and shut the door behind him.

Another dead silence fell upon the group. Then a citizen on the other side of the stove, by the aid of his elbows, lifted himself perpendicularly, unhooked a coat from a peg, and remarked to himself in a tone that expressed supreme disgust: —

"Please him! In a pig's eye it will," and disappeared into the night.

Only two loungers were now left — the butternut man with the sinister expression, and the red-faced man with the dyed mustache.

The landlord for the second time dropped into a chair beside me.

"I knowed Dick was out, but I did n't say nothing, so many of these fellers 'round here is down on him. The night his time was up Dick come in here on his way home and asked after his mother. He had n't heard from her for a month, and was nigh worried to death about her. I told him she was all right, and had him in to dinner. He'd fleshed up a bit and nobody did n't catch on who he was, — bein' away nigh five years, — and so I passed him off for a drummer."

At this the red-faced man who had been tilted back, his feet on the iron rod encircling the stove, brought them down with a bang, stretched his arms above his head, and said with a yawn, addressing the pots of geraniums on the window sill, "Them as likes jail-birds can have jail-birds," and lounged out of the room, followed by the citizen in butternut. It was apparent that the supper hour of the group had arrived. It was equally evident that the hospitality of the fireside did not extend to the table.

"You heard that fellow, did n't you?" said the landlord, turning to me after a moment's pause. "You 'd think to hear him talk there warn't nobody honest 'round here but him. That 's Chris Rankin — he keeps a rum mill up to the Forks and sells tanglefoot and groceries to the miners. By Sunday mornin' he 's got 'bout every cent they 've earned. There ain't a woman in the settlement would n't be glad if somebody would break his head. I 'd rather be Dick Sands than him. Dick never drank a drop in his life, and won't let nobody else if he can help it.

That 's what that slouch hates him for, and that 's what he hates me for."

The landlord spoke with some feeling — so much so that I squared my chair and faced him to listen the better. His last remark, too, explained a sign tacked over the desk reading, "No liquors sold here," and which had struck me as unusual when I entered.

"What was this man's crime?" I asked. "There seems to be some difference of opinion about him."

"His crime, neighbor, was because there was a lot of fellers that did n't have no common sense — that 's what his crime was. I 've known Dick since he was knee-high to a barrel o' taters, and there warn't no better" —

"But he was sent up the second time," I interrupted, glancing at my watch. "So the driver said." I had not the slightest interest in Mr. Richard Sands, his crimes or misfortunes.

"Yes, and they 'd sent him up the third time if Judge Polk had lived. The first time it was a pocket-book and three dollars, and the second time it was a ham. Polk did that. Polk 's dead now. God help him if he 'd been alive when Dick got out the last time. First question he asked me after I told him his mother was all right was whether 't was true

Polk was dead. When I told him he was he did n't say nothin' at first — just looked down on the floor and then he said slow-like :—

"'If Polk had had any common sense, Uncle Jimmy,' — he always calls me 'Uncle Jimmy,' — 'he 'd saved himself a heap o' worry and me a good deal o' sufferin'. I 'm glad he 's dead.'"

II

THE driver arrived on the minute, backed up to the sprawling wooden steps, and kicked open the door of the waiting-room with his foot.

"All right, boss, I got two passengers 'stead o' one, but you won't kick, I know. You git in ; I 'll go for the mail." The promotion and the confidential tone were intended as a compliment.

I slipped into my fur overcoat ; slid my manuscript into the outside pocket, and followed the driver out into the cold night. The only light visible came from a smoky kerosene lamp boxed in at the far end of the stage and protected by a pane of glass labeled in red paint, "Fare, ten cents."

Close to its rays sat a man, and close to

the man — so close that I mistook her for an overcoat thrown over his arm — cuddled a little girl, the light of the lamp falling directly on her face. She was about ten years of age, and wore a cheap woolen hood tied close to her face, and a red shawl crossed over her chest and knotted behind her back. Her hair was yellow and weather-burned, as if she had played out of doors all her life; her eyes were pale blue, and her face freckled. Neither she nor the man made any answer to my salutation.

The child looked up into the man's face and shrugged her shoulders with a slight shiver. The man drew her closer to him, as if to warm her the better, and felt her chapped red hands. In the movement his face came into view. He was, perhaps, thirty years of age — wiry and well built, with an oval face ending in a pointed Vandyke beard; piercing brown eyes, finely chiseled nose, and a well-modeled mouth over which drooped a blond mustache. He was dressed in a dark blue flannel shirt, with loose sailor collar tied with a red 'kerchief, and a black, stiff-brimmed army-shaped hat a little drawn down over his eyes. Buttoned over his chest was a heavy waistcoat made of a white and gray deerskin, with the hair on the outside. His trousers, which fitted snugly his slender, shapely legs, were tucked into his boots. He wore no coat, despite the cold.

A typical young westerner, I said to myself — one of the bone and sinew of the land — accustomed to live anywhere in these mountains — cold proof, of course, or he'd wear a coat on a night like this. Taking his little sister home, I suppose. The country will never go to the dogs as long as we have these young fellows to fall back upon. Then my eyes rested with pleasure on the pointed beard, the peculiar curve of the hat-brim, the slender waist corrugating the soft fur of the deerskin waistcoat, and the peculiar set of his trousers and boots — like those of an Austrian on parade. And how picturesque, I thought. What an admirable costume for the ideal cowboy or the romantic mountain ranger who comes in at the nick of time to save the young maiden; and what a hit the favorite of the footlights would make if he could train his physique down to such wire-drawn, alert, panther-like outlines and —

A heavy object struck the boot of the stage and interrupted my meditations. It was the mail-bag. The next instant the driver's head was thrust in the door.

"Dick, this is the man I told you was goin'

'long far as Bingville. He 's got a show up to the college."

I started, hardly believing my ears. Shades of D'Artagnan, Davy Crockett, and Daniel Boone! Could this lithe, well-knit, brown-eyed young Robin Hood be a convict?

"Are you Dick Sands?" I faltered out.

"Yes, that 's what they call me when I 'm out of jail. When I 'm in I 'm known as One Hundred and Two."

He spoke calmly, quite as if I had asked him his age — the voice clear and low, with a certain cadence that surprised me all the more. His answer, too, convinced me that the driver had told him of my time-honored views on solitary confinement, and that it had disposed him to be more or less frank toward me. If he expected, however, any further outburst of sympathy from me he was disappointed. The surprise had been so great, and the impression he had made upon me so favorable, that it would have been impossible for me to remind him even in the remotest way of his former misfortunes.

The child looked at me with her pale eyes, and crept still closer, holding on to the man's arm, steadying herself as the stage bumped over the crossings.

For some minutes I kept still, my topics

of conversation especially adapted to convicts being limited. Despite my implied boasting to the driver, I had never, to my knowledge, met one before. Then, again, I had not yet adjusted my mind to the fact that the man before me had ever worn stripes. So I said, aimlessly: —

"Is that your little sister?"

"No, I have n't got any little sister," still in the same calm voice. "This is Ben Mulford's girl; she lives next to me, and I am taking her down for the ride. She 's coming back."

The child's hand stole along the man's knee, found his fingers and held on. I kept silence for a while, wondering what I would say next. I felt that to a certain extent I was this man's guest, and therefore under obligation to preserve the amenities. I began again: —

"The driver tells me your mother 's sick?"

"Yes, she is. She went over to her sister's last week and got cold. She is n't what she was — I being away from her so much lately. I got two terms; last time for five years. Every little thing now knocks her out."

He raised his head and looked at me calmly — all over — examining each detail, —

my derby hat, white tie, fur overcoat, along my arms to my gloves, and slowly down to my shoes.

"I s'pose you never done no time?" He had no suspicion that I had; he only meant to be amiable.

"No," I said, with equal simplicity, meeting him on his own ground — quite as if an attack of measles at some earlier age was under discussion, to which he had fallen a victim while I had escaped. As he spoke his fingers tightened over the child's hand. Then he turned and straightened her hood, tucking the loose strands of hair under its edge with his fingers.

"You seem rather fond of that little girl; is she any relation?" I asked, forgetting that I had asked almost that same question before.

"No, she is n't any relation — just Ben Mulford's girl." He raised his other hand and pressed the child's head down upon the deerskin waistcoat, close into the fur, with infinite tenderness. The child reached up her small, chapped hand and laid it on his cheek, cuddling closer, a shy, satisfied smile overspreading her face.

My topics were exhausted, and we rode on in silence, he sitting in front of me, his eyes now so completely hidden in the shadow of his broad-brimmed hat that I only knew they were fixed on me when some sudden tilt of the stage threw the light full on his face. I tried offering him a cigar, but he would not smoke — "had gotten out of the habit of it," he said, "being shut up so long. It did n't taste good to him, so he had given it up."

When the stage reached the crossing near the college gate and stopped, he asked quietly: —

"You get out here?" and lifted the child as he spoke so that her soiled shoes would not scrape my coat. In the action I saw that his leg pained him, for he bent it suddenly and put his hand on the kneecap.

"I hope your mother will be better," I said. "Good-night; good-night, little girl."

"Thank you; good-night," he answered quickly, with a strain of sadness that I had not caught before. The child raised her eyes to mine, but did not speak.

I mounted the hill to the big college building, and stopped under a light to look back, following with my eyes the stage on its way to the station. The child was on her knees, looking at me out of the window and waving her hand, but the man sat by the lamp, his head on his chest.

. . . .

All through my discourse the picture of that keen-eyed, handsome young fellow, with his pointed beard and picturesque deerskin waistcoat, the little child cuddled down upon his breast, kept coming before me.

When I had finished, and was putting on my coat in the president's room, — the landlord had sent his team to bring me back, — I asked one of the professors, a dry, crackling, sandy-haired professor, with bulging eyes and watch-crystal spectacles, if he knew of a man by the name of Sands who had lived in Hell's Diggings with his mother, and who had served two terms in state's prison, and I related my experience in the stage, telling him of the impression his face and bearing had made upon me, and of his tenderness to the child beside him.

"No, my dear sir, I never heard of him. Hell's Diggings is a most unsafe and unsavory locality. I would advise you to be very careful in returning. The rogue will probably be lying in wait to rob you of your fee;" and he laughed a little harsh laugh that sounded as if some one had suddenly torn a coarse rag.

"But the child with him," I said; "he seemed to love her."

"That 's no argument, my dear sir. If he has been twice in state's prison he probably belongs to that class of degenerates in whom all moral sense is lacking. I have begun making some exhaustive investigations of the data obtainable on this subject, which I have embodied in a report, and which I propose sending to the State Committee on the treatment of criminals, and which" —

"Do you know any criminals personally?" I asked blandly, cutting short, as I could see, an extract from the report. His manner, too, strange to say, rather nettled me.

"Thank God, no, sir; not one! Do you?"

"I am not quite sure," I answered. "I thought I had, but I may have been mistaken."

III

WHEN I again mounted the sprawling steps of the disheartened-looking tavern, the landlord was sitting by the stove half asleep and alone. He had prepared a little supper, he said, as he led the way, with a benign smile, into the dining-room, where a lonely bracket lamp, backed by a tin reflector, revealed a table holding a pitcher of milk, a saucer of preserves, and some pieces of leather beef about the size used in repairing shoes.

"Come, and sit down by me," I said. "I want to talk to you about this young fellow Sands. Tell me everything you know."

"Well, you saw him; clean and pert-lookin', ain't he? Don't look much like a habitual criminal, as Polk called him, does he?"

"No, he certainly does not; but give me the whole story." I was in a mood either to reserve decision or listen to a recommendation of mercy.

"Want me to tell you about the pocket-book or that ham scrape?"

"Everything from the beginning," and I reached for the scraps of beef and poured out a glass of milk.

"Well, you saw Chris Rankin, did n't you, — that fellow that talked about jail-birds? Well, one night about six or seven years ago," — the landlord had now drawn out a chair from the other side of the table and was sitting opposite me, leaning forward, his arms on the cloth, — "maybe six years ago, a jay of a farmer stopped at Rankin's and got himself plumb full o' tanglefoot. When he come to pay he hauled out a wallet and chucked it over to Chris and told him to take it out. The wallet struck the edge of the counter and fell on the floor, and out come a wad o' bills. The only other man besides him and Chris in the bar-room was Dick. It was Saturday night, and Dick had come in to git his paper, which was always left to Rankin's. Dick seen he was drunk, and he picked the wallet up and handed it back to the farmer. About an hour after that the farmer come a-runnin' in to Rankin's sober as a deacon, a-hollerin' that he 'd been robbed, and wanted to know where Dick was. He said that he had had two rolls o' bills; one was in an envelope with three dollars in it that he 'd got from the bank, and the other was the roll he paid Chris with. Dick, he claimed, was the last man who had handled the wallet, and he vowed he 'd stole the envelone with the three dollars when he handed it back to him.

"When the trial come off everything went dead ag'in Dick. The cashier of the bank swore he had given the farmer the money and envelope, and in three new one-dollar bills of the bank, mind you, for the farmer had sold some ducks for his wife and wanted clean money for her. Chris swore he seen Dick pick it up and fix the money all straight again for the farmer; the farmer's wife swore she had took the money out of her husband's pocket, and that when she opened the wallet the envelope was gone, and the farmer, who was so dumb he could n't write his name, swore that he had n't stopped no place between Chris Rankin's and home, 'cept just a minute to fix his traces t'other side of Big Pond Woods.

"Dick's mother, of course, was nigh crazy, and she come to me and I went and got Lawyer White. It come up 'fore Judge Polk. After we had all swore to Dick's good character and, mind you, there warn't one of 'em could say a word ag'in him 'cept that he lived in Hell's Diggin's, Lawyer White began his speech, clamin' that Dick had always been square as a brick, and that the money must be found on Dick or somewheres nigh him 'fore they could prove he took it.

"Well, the jury was the kind we always git 'round here, and they done what Polk told 'em to in his charge, — just as they always do, — and Dick was found guilty before them fellers left their seats. The mother give a shriek and fell in a heap on the floor, but Dick never changed a muscle nor said a word. When Polk asked him if he had anything to say, he stood up and turned his back on Polk, and faced the court-room, which was jam full, for everybody knowed him and everybody liked him — you could n't help it.

"'You people have knowed me here,' Dick says, 'since I was a boy, and you 've knowed my mother. I ain't never in times back done nothin' I was ashamed of, and I ain't now, and you know it. I tell you, men, I did n't take that money.' Then he faced the jury. 'I don't know,' he said, 'as I blame you. Most of you don't know no better and those o' you who do are afraid to say it; but you, Judge Polk,' and he squared himself and pointed his finger straight at him, 'you claim to be a man of eddication, and so there ain't no excuse for you. You 've seen me grow up here, and if you had any common sense you 'd know that a man like me could n't steal that man's money, and you 'd know, too, that he was too drunk to know what had become of it.' Then he stopped and said in a low voice, and with his teeth set, looking right into Polk's eyes: 'Now I 'm ready to take whatever you choose to give me, but remember one thing, I 'll settle with you if I ever come back for puttin' this misery on to my mother, and don't you forget it.'

"Polk got a little white about the gills, but he give Dick a year, and they took him away to Stoneburg.

"After that the mother ran down and got poorer and poorer, and folks avoided her, and she got behind and had to sell her stuff, and a month before his time was out she got sick and pretty near died. Dick went straight home and never left her day nor night, and just stuck to her and nursed her like any girl would a-done, and got her well again. Of course folks was divided, and it got red-hot 'round here. Some believed him innercent, and some believed him guilty. Lawyer White and fellers like him stuck to him, but Rankin's gang was down on him; and when he come into Chris's place for his paper same as before, all the bums that hang 'round there got up and left, and Chris told Dick he did n't want him there no more. That kinder broke the boy's heart, though he did n't say nothing, and after that he would go off up in the woods by himself, or he 'd go huntin' ches'-nuts or picking flowers, all the children after him. Every child in the settlement loved him, and could n't stay away from him. Queer, ain't it, how folks would trust their chil'ren. All the folks in Hell's Diggin's did, anyhow."

"Yes," I interrupted, "there was one with him to-night in the stage."

"That 's right. He always has one or two boys and girls 'long with him; says nothin' ain't honest, no more, 'cept chil'ren and dogs.

"Well, when his mother got 'round ag'in all right, Dick started in to get something to do. He could n't get nothin' here, so he went acrost the mountains to Castleton and got work in a wagon fact'ry. When it come pay day and they asked him his name he said out loud, Dick Sands, of Hell's Diggin's. This give him away, and the men would n't work with him, and he had to go. I see him the mornin' he got back. He come in and asked for me, and I went out, and he said, 'Uncle Jimmy, they mean I sha'n't work 'round here. They won't give me no work, and when I git it they won't let me stay. Now, by God!'—and he slammed his fist down on the desk—'they 'll support me and my mother without workin',' and he went out.

"Next thing I heard Dick had come into Rankin's and picked up a ham and walked off with it. Chris, he allus 'lowed, hurt him worse than any one else around here, and so maybe he determined to begin on him. Chris was standin' at the bar when he picked up the ham, and he grabbed a gun and started for him. Dick waited a-standin' in the road, and just as Chris was a-pullin' the trigger, he jumped at him, plantin' his fist in 'tween Chris's eyes. Then he took his gun and went off with the ham. Chris did n't come to for an hour. Then Dick barricaded himself in his house, put his mother in the cellar, strung a row of cartridges 'round his waist, and told 'em to come on. Well, his mother plead with him not to do murder, and after a day he give himself up and come out.

"At the trial the worst scared man was Polk. Dick had dropped in on him once or twice after he got out, tellin' him how he could n't git no work and askin' him to speak up and set him straight with the folks. They do say that Polk never went out o' night when Dick was home, 'fraid he 'd waylay him — though I knew Polk was givin' himself a good deal of worry for nothin', for Dick warn't the kind to hit a man on the sly. When Polk see who it was a-comin' into court he called the constable and asked if Dick had been searched, and when he found he had he told Ike Martin, the constable, to stand near the bench in case the prisoner got ugly.

"But Dick never said a word, 'cept to say he took the ham and he never intended to pay for it, and he 'd take it again whenever his mother was hungry.

"So Polk give him five years, sayin' it was his second offense, and that he was a 'habitual criminal.' It was all over in half an hour, and Ike Martin and the sheriff had Dick in a buggy and on the way to Stoneburg. They reached the jail about nine o'clock at night, and drove up to the gate. Well, sir, Ike got out on one side and the sheriff he got out on t'other, so they could get close to him when he got down, and, by gosh! 'fore they knowed where they was at, Dick give a spring clear over the dashboard and that 's the last they see of him for two months. One day, after they 'd hunted him high and low and lay 'round his mother's cabin, and jumped in on her half a dozen times in the middle of the night, hopin' to get him, — for Polk had offered a reward of five hundred dollars, dead or alive, — Ike come in to my place all het up and his eyes a-hangin' out, and he say, 'Gimme your long gun, quick, we got Dick Sands.' I says, 'How do you know?' and he says, 'Some boys seen smoke comin' out of a mineral hole half a mile up the mountain above Hell's Diggin's, and Dick 's in there with a bed and blanket, and we 're goin' to lay for him to-night and plug him when he comes out if he don't surrender.' And I says, 'You can't have no gun o' mine to shoot Dick, and if I knowed where he was I 'd go tell him.' The room was full when he asked for my gun, and some o' the boys from Hell's Diggin's heard him and slid off through the woods, and when the sheriff and his men got there they see the smoke still comin' up, and lay in the bushes all night watchin'. 'Bout an hour after daylight they crep' up. The fire was out and so was Dick, and all they found was a chicken half cooked and a quilt off his mother's bed.

"'Bout a week after that, one Saturday night, a feller come runnin' up the street from the market, sayin' Dick had walked into his place just as he was closin' up, — he had a stall in the public market under the city hall, where the court is, — and asked him polite as you please for a cup of coffee and a piece of bread, and before he could holler Dick was off again with the bread under his arm. Well, of course, nobody did n't believe him, for they knowed Dick warn't darn fool enough to be loafin' 'round a place within twenty foot of the room where Polk sentenced him. Some said the feller was crazy, and some said it was a put-up job to throw Ike and the others off the scent. But the next night Dick, with his gun handy in the hollow of his arm, and his hat cocked over his eye, stepped up to the cook shop in the corner of the market and helped himself to a pie and a chunk o' cheese right under their very eyes, and 'fore they could say ‘scat,’ he was off ag’in and did n’t leave no more tracks than a cat.

“By this time the place was wild. Fellers was gettin’ their guns, and Ike Martin was runnin’ here and there organizing posses, and most every other man you ’d meet had a gun and was swore in as a deputy to git Dick and some of the five hundred dollars’ reward. They hung ’round the market, and they patrolled the streets, and they had signs and countersigns, and more tomfoolery than would run a circus. Dick lay low and never let on, and nobody did n’t see him for another week, when a farmer comin’ in with milk ’bout daylight had the life pretty nigh scared out o’ him by Dick stopping him, sayin’ he was thirsty, and then liftin’ the lid off the tin without so much as ‘by your leave,’ and takin’ his fill of the can. ’Bout a week after that the rope got tangled up in the belfry over the court-house so they could n’t ring for fires, and the janitor went up to fix it, and when he came down his legs was shakin’ so he could n’t stand. What do you think he ’d found?” And the landlord leaned over and broke out in a laugh, striking the table with the flat of his hand until every plate and tumbler rattled.

I made no answer.

"By gosh, there was Dick sound asleep! He had a bed and blankets and lots o' provisions, and was just as comfortable as a bug in a rug. He 'd been there ever since he got out of the mineral hole! Tell you I got to laugh whenever I think of it. Dick laughed 'bout it himself t'other day when he told me what fun he had listenin' to Ike and the deputies plannin' to catch him. There ain't another man around here who 'd been smart enough to pick out the belfry. He was right over the room in the court-house where they was, ye see, and he could look down 'tween the cracks and hear every word they said. Rainy nights he 'd sneak out, and his mother would come down to the market, and he 'd see her outside. They never tracked her, of course, when she come there. He told me she wanted him to go clean away somewheres, but he would n't leave her.

"When the janitor got his breath he busted in on Ike and the others sittin' 'round swappin' lies how they 'd catch Dick, and Ike reached for his gun and crep' up the ladder with two deputies behind him, and Ike was so scared and so 'fraid he 'd lose the money that he fired 'fore Dick got on his feet. The ball broke his leg, and they all jumped in and clubbed him over the head and carried him downstairs for dead in his blankets, and laid him on a butcher's table in the market, and all the folks in the market crowded 'round to look at him, lyin' there with his head hangin' down over the table like a stuck calf's, and his clothes all bloody. Then Ike handcuffed him and started for Stoneburg in a wagon 'fore Dick come to."

"That's why he could n't walk to-night," I asked, "and why the driver took him over in the stage?"

"Yes, that was it. He 'll never get over it. Sometimes he 's all right, and then ag'in it hurts him terrible, 'specially when the weather 's bad.

"All the time he was up to Stoneburg them last four years — he got a year off for good behavior — he kept makin' little things and sellin' 'em to the visitors. Everybody went to his cell — it was the first place the warders took 'em, and they all bought things from Dick. He had a nice word for everybody, kind and comforting-like. He was the handiest feller you ever see. When he got out he had twenty-nine dollars. He give every cent to his mother. Warden told him when he left he had n't had no better man in the prison since he had been 'p'inted. And there ain't no better feller now. It 's a darned mean shame how Chris Rankin and them fellers is down on him, knowin', too, how it all turned out."

I leaned back in my chair and looked at the landlord. I was conscious of a slight choking in my throat which could hardly be traced to the dryness of the beef. I was conscious, too, of a peculiar affection of the eyes. Two or three lamps seemed to be swimming around the room, and one or more blurred landlords were talking to me with elbows on tables.

"What do you think yourself about that money of the farmer's?" I asked automatically, though I do not think even now that I had the slightest suspicion of his guilt. "Do you believe he stole the three dollars when he handed the wallet back?"

"Stole 'em? Not by a d—— sight! Did n't I tell you? Thought I had. That galoot of a farmer dropped it in the woods 'longside the road when he got out to fix his traces, and he was too full of Chris Rankin's rum to remember it, and after Dick had been sent up for the second time, the second time now, mind ye, and had been in two years for walking off with Rankin's ham, a lot of school children huntin' for ches'nuts come upon that same envelope in the ditch with them three new dollars in it, covered up under the leaves and the weeds a-growin' over it. Ben Mulford's girl found it."

"What, the child he had with him tonight?"

"Yes, little freckle-faced girl with white eyes. Oh, I tell you Dick's awful fond of that kid."

A KENTUCKY CINDERELLA

I WAS bending over my easel, hard at work upon a full-length portrait of a young girl in a costume of fifty years ago, when the door of my studio opened softly and Aunt Chloe came in.

"Good-mawnin', suh! I did n' think you 'd come to-day, bein' a Sunday," she said, with a slight bend of her knees. "I 'll jes' sweep up a lil mite; doan' ye move, I won't 'sturb ye."

Aunt Chloe had first opened my door a year before with a note from Marny, a brother brush, which began with "Here is an old Southern mammy who has seen better days; paint her if you can," and ended with, "Any way, give her a job."

The bearer of the note was indeed the ideal mammy, even to the bandanna handkerchief bound about her head, and the capacious waist and ample bosom — the lullaby resting-place for many a child, white and black. I had never seen a real one in the flesh before. I had heard about them in my earlier days. Daddy Billy, my father's body servant and my father's slave, who lived to be ninety-four, had told me of his own Aunt Mirey, who had died in the old days, but too far back for me to remember. And I had listened, when a boy, to the traditions connected with the plantations of my ancestors, — of the Keziahs and Mammy Crouches and Mammy Janes, — but I had never looked into the eyes of one of the old school until I saw Aunt Chloe, nor had I ever fully realized how quaintly courteous and gentle one of them could be until, with an old-time manner, born of a training seldom found outside of the old Southern homes, she bent forward, spread her apron with both hands, and with a little backward dip had said as she left me that first day: "Thank ye, suh! I 'll come eve'y Sunday mawnin'. I 'll do my best to please ye, an' I specs I kin."

I do not often work on Sunday, but my picture had been too long delayed waiting for a faded wedding dress worn once by the original when she was a bride, and which had only been found when two of her descendants had ransacked their respective garrets.

"Mus' be mighty driv, suh," she said, "a-workin' on de Sabbath day. Golly, but dat 's a purty lady!" and she put down her pail. "I see it las' Sunday when I come in, but she did n't had dem ruffles 'round her neck

AUNT CHLOE

den dat you done gib her. 'Clar' to goodness, dat chile look like she was jes' a-gwine to speak."

Aunt Chloe was leaning on her broom, her eyes scrutinizing the portrait.

"Well, if dat doan' beat de lan'. I ain't never seen none o' dem frocks since de ole times. An' dem lil low shoes wid de ribbons crossed on de ankles! She's de livin' pussonecation — she is so, for a fac'. Uhm! Uhm!" (It is difficult to convey this peculiar sound of complete approval in so many letters.)

"Did you ever know anybody like her?" I asked.

The old woman straightened her back, and for a moment her eyes looked into mine. I had often tried to draw from her something of her earlier life, but she had always evaded my questions. Marny had told me that his attempts had at first been equally disappointing.

"Body as ole 's me, suh, seen a plenty o' people." Then her eyes sought the canvas again.

After a moment's pause she said, as if to herself: "You 's de real quality, chile, dat you is; eve'y spec an' spinch o' ye."

I tried again.

"Does it look like anybody you ever saw, Aunt Chloe?"

"It do an' it don't," she answered critically. "De feet is like hern, but de eyes ain't."

"Who?"

"Oh, Miss Nannie." And she leaned again on her broom and looked down on the floor.

I heaped up a little pile of pigments on one corner of my palette and flattened them for a high light on a fold in the satin gown.

"Who was Miss Nannie?" I asked carelessly. I was afraid the thread would break if I pulled too hard.

"One o' my chillen, honey." A peculiar softness came into her voice.

"Tell me about her. It will help me get her eyes right, so you can remember her better. They don't look human enough to me anyhow" (this last to myself). "Where did she live?"

"Where dey all live — down in de big house. She warn't Marse Henry's real chile, but she come o' de blood. She did n't hab dem kind o' shoes on her footses when I fust see her, but she wore 'em when she lef' me. Dat she did." Her voice rose suddenly and her eyes brightened. "An' dem ain't nothin' to de way dey shined. I ain't never seen no satin slippers shine like dem slippers; dey was jes' ablaze!"

I worked on in silence. Marny had cautioned me not to be too curious. Some day she might open her heart and tell me wonderful stories of her earlier life, but I must not appear too anxious. She had become rather suspicious of strangers since she had moved North and lost track of her own people, Marny had said.

Aunt Chloe picked up her pail and began moving some easels into a far corner of my studio and piling the chairs in a heap. This done, she stopped again and stood behind me, looking intently at the canvas over my shoulder.

"My! My! ain't dat de ve'y image of dat frock? I kin see it now jes' as Miss Nannie come down de stairs. But you got to put dat gold chain on it 'fore it gits to be de ve'y 'spress image. I had it roun' my own neck once; I know jes' how it looked."

I laid down my palette, and picking up a piece of chalk asked her to describe it so that I could make an outline.

"It was long an' heavy, an' it woun' roun' de neck twice an' hung down to de wais'. An' dat watch on de end of it! Well, I ain't seen none like dat one sence. I 'clar' to ye it was jes' 's teeny as one o' dem lil biscuits I used to make for 'er when she come in de kitchen — an' she was dere most of de time. Dey did n't care nuffin for her much. Let 'er go roun' barefoot half de time, an' her hair a-flyin'. Only one good frock to her name, an' dat warn't nuffin but calico. I used to wash dat many a time for her long 'fore she was outen her bed. Allus makes my blood bile to dis day whenever I think of de way dey treated dat chile. But it did n't make no diff'ence what she had on — shoes or no shoes — her footses was dat lil. An' purty! Wid her big eyes an' her cheeks jes' 's fresh as dem rosewater roses dat I used to snip off for ole Sam to put on de table. Oh! I tell ye, if ye could picter her like dat dey would n't be nobody clear from here to glory could come nigh her."

Aunt Chloe's eyes were kindling with every word. I remembered Marny's warning and kept still. I had abandoned the sketch of the chain as an unnecessary incentive, and had begun again with my palette knife, pottering away, nodding appreciatingly, and now and then putting a question to clear up some tangled situation as to dates and localities which her rambling talk had left unsettled.

"Yes, suh, down in the blue grass country, near Lexin'ton, Kentucky, whar my ole master, Marse Henry Gordon, lived," she answered to my inquiry as to where this all happened. "I used to go eve'y year to see him after de war was over, an' kep' it up till he died. Dere warn't nobody like him den, an' dere ain't none now. He warn't never spiteful to chillen, white or black. Eve'ybody knowed dat. I was a pickaninny mysc'f, an' I b'longed to him. An' he ain't never laid a lick on me, an' he would n't let nobody else do 't nuther, 'cept my mammy. I 'members one time when Aunt Dinah made cake dat ole Sam — he war a heap younger den — could n't put it on de table 'ca'se dere was a piece broke out'n it. Sam he riz, an' Dinah she riz, an' after dey 'd called each other all de names dey could lay dere tongues to, Miss Ann, my own fust mist'ess, come in an' she say dem chillen tuk dat cake, an' 't ain't nary one o' ye dat 's 'sponsible.' 'What 's dis,' says Marse Henry — 'chillen stealin' cake? Send 'em here to me!' When we all come in — dere was six or eight of us — he says, 'Eve'y one o' ye look me in de eye; now which one tuk it?' I kep' lookin' away, — fust on de flo' an' den out de windy. 'Look at me,' he says agin. 'You ain't lookin', Clorindy.' Den I cotched him watchin' me. 'Now you all go out,' he says, 'and de one dat 's guilty kin come back agin.' Den we all went out in de yard. 'You tell him,' says one. 'No, you tell him;' an' dat 's de way it went on. I knowed I was de wustest, for I opened de door o' de sideboard an' gin it to de others. Den I thought, if I don't tell him mebbe he 'll lick de whole passel on us, an' dat ain't right; but if I go tell him an' beg his 'umble pardon he might lemme go. So I crep' 'round where he was a-settin' wid his book on his knee," — Aunt Chloe was now moving stealthily behind me, her eyes fixed on her imaginary master, head down, one finger in her mouth, — "an' I say, 'Marse Henry!' An' he look up an' say, 'Who 's dat?' An' I say, 'Dat 's Clorindy.' An' he say, 'What you want?' 'Marse Henry, I come to tell ye I was hungry, an' I see de door open an' I shove it back an' tuk de piece o' cake, an' maybe I thought if I done tole ye you 'd forgib me.'

"'Den you is de ringleader,' he says, 'an' you tempted de other chillen?' 'Yes,' I says, 'I spec so.' 'Well,' he says, lookin' down on de carpet, 'now dat you has perfessed an' beg pardon, you is good an' ready to pay 'tention to what I 'm gwine to say.' De other chillen had sneaked up an' was listenin'; dey 'spected to see me git it, though dere ain't nary one of 'em ever knowed him to strike 'em a lick. Den he says: 'Dis here is a lil thing, — dis stealin a cake; an' it's a big thing at de same time. Miss Ann has been right smart put out 'bout it, an' I'm gwine to see dat it don't happen agin. If you see a pin on de fl'or you would n't steal it, — you'd pick it up if you wanted it, an' it would n't be nuffin, 'cause somebody th'owed it away an' it was free to eve'body; but if you see a piece o' money on de fl'or, you knowed nobody did n't th'ow dat away, an' if you pick it up an' don't tell, dat's somethin' else — dat's stealin', 'cause you tuk somethin' dat somebody else has paid somethin' for an' dat belongs to him. Now dis cake ain't o' much 'count, but it warn't yourn, an' you ought n't to ha' tuk it. If you'd asked yo'r mist'ess for it she'd gin you a piece. There ain't nuffin here you chillen doan' git when ye ask for it.' I did n't say nuffin more. I jes' waited for him to do anythin' he wanted to me. Den he looks at de carpet for a long time an' he says: —

"'I reckon you won't take no mo' cake 'thout askin' for it, Clorindy, an' you chillen kin go out an' play agin.'"

The tears were now standing in her eyes.

"Dat 's what my ole master was, suh; I ain't never forgot it. If he had beat me to death he could n't 'a' done no mo' for me. He jes' splained to me an' I ain't never forgot since."

"Did your own mother find it out?" I asked.

The tears were gone now; her face was radiant again at my question.

"Dat she did, suh. One o' de chillen done tole on me. Mammy jes' made one grab as I run pas' de kitchen door, an' reached for a barrel stave, an' she fairly sot — me — afire!"

Aunt Chloe was now holding her sides with laughter, fresh tears streaming down her cheeks.

"But Marse Henry never knowed it. Lawd, suh, dere ain't nobody round here like him, nor never was. I kin 'member him now same as it was yisterday, wid his white hair, an' he a-settin' in his big chair. It was de las' time I ever see him. De big house was gone, an' de colored people was gone, an' he was dat po' he did n't know where de nex' mouf'ful was a-comin' from. I come out behind him so," — Aunt Chloe made me her old master and my stool his rocking-chair, — "an' I pat him on the shoulder dis way, an' he say, 'Chloe, is dat you? How is it yo' looks so comf'ble like?' An' I say, 'It 's you, Marse Henry; you done it all; yo' teachin' made me what I is, an' if you study about it you 'll know it 's so. An' de others ain't no wus'. Of all de colored people you owned, dere ain't nary one been hung, or been in de penitentiary, nor ain't knowed as liars. Dat 's de way you fotch us up.'

"An' I love him yet, an' if he was a-livin' to-day I 'd work for him an' take care of him if I went hungry myse'f. De only fool thing Marster Henry ever done was a-marryin' dat widow woman for his second wife. Miss Nannie, dat looks a lil bit like dat chile you got dere before ye" — and she pointed to the canvas — "would n't a been sot on an' 'bused like she was but for her. Dat woman warn't nuffin but a harf-strainer noway, if I do say it. Eve'body knowed dat. How Marse Henry Gordon come to marry her nobody don't know till dis day. She warn't none o' our people. Dey do say dat he met her up to Frankfort when he was in de Legislater, but I don't know if dat 's so. But she warn't nuffin, nohow."

"Was Miss Nannie her child?" I asked,

stepping back from my easel to get the better effect of my canvas.

"No suh, dat she warn't!" with emphasis. "She was Marse Henry's own sister's chile, she was. Her people — Miss Nannie's — lived up in Indiany, an' dey was jes 's po' as watermelon rinds, and when her mother died Marse Henry sent for her to come live wid him, 'cause he said Miss Rachel — dat was dat woman's own chile by her fust husband — was lonesome. Dey was bofe about de one age, — fo'teen or fifteen years old, — but Lawd-a-massy! Miss Rachel warn't lonesome 'cept for what she could n't git, an' she most broke her heart 'bout dat, much 's she could break it 'bout anything.

"I remember de ve'y day Miss Nannie come. I see her comin' down de road totin' a big ban'box, an' a carpet bag mos 's big 's herse'f. Den she turned in de gate. ''Fo' God,' I says to ole Sam, who was settin' de table for dinner, 'who 's dis yere comin' in?' Den I see her stop an' set de bundles down an' catch her bref, and den she come on agin.

"'Dat 's Marse Henry's niece,' he says. 'I heared de mist'ess say she was a-comin' one day dis week by de coach.'

"I see right away dat dat woman was up to one of her tricks; she did n't 'tend to let dat chile come no other way 'cept like a servant; she was dat dirt mean.

"Oh, you need n't look, suh! I ain't meanin' no onrespect, but I knowed dat woman when Marse Henry fust married her, an' she ain't never fooled me once. Fust time she come into de house she walked plumb in de kitchen, where me an' old Sam an' ole Dinah was a-eaten our dinner, we setten at de table like we useter did, and she flung her head up in de air and she says: 'After dis when I come in I want you niggers to git up on yo' feet.' Think o' dat, will ye? Marse Henry never called nary one of us nigger since we was pickaninnies. I knowed den she warn't 'customed to nuthin'. But I tell ye she never put on dem kind o' airs when Marse Henry was about. No, suh. She was always mighty sugar-like to him when he was home, but dere ain't no conniption she warn't up to when he could n't hear of it. She had purty nigh riz de roof when he done tell her dat Miss Nannie was a-comin' to live wid 'em, but she could n't stand agin him, for warn't her only daughter, Miss Rachel, livin' on him, an' not only Miss Rachel, but lots mo' of her people where she come from?

"Well, suh, as soon as ole Sam said what chile it was dat was a-comin' down de road I dropped my dishcloth an' I run out to meet 'er.

"'Is you Miss Nannie?' I says. 'Gimme dat bag,' I says, 'an' dat box.'

"'Yes,' she says, 'dat 's me, an' ain't you Aunt Chloe what I heared so much about?'

"Honey, you ain't never gwine to git de kind o' look on dat picter you 's workin' on dere, suh, as sweet as dat chile's face when she said dat to me. I loved her from dat fust minute I see her, an' I loved her ever since, jes' as I loved her mother befo' her.

"When she got to de house, me a-totin' de things on behind, de mist'ess come out on de po'ch.

"'Oh, dat 's you, is it, Nannie?' she says. 'Well, Chloe 'll tell ye where to go,' an' she went straight in de house agin. Never kissed her, nor touched her, nor nuffin!

"Ole Sam was bilin'. He heard her say it, an' if he was alive he 'd tell ye same as me.

"'Where 's she gwine to sleep?' I says, callin' after her; 'upstairs long wid Miss Rachel?' I was gittin' hot myse'f, though I did n't say nuffin.

"'No,' she says, flingin' up her head like a goat; 'my daughter needs all de room she 's got. You kin take her downstairs an' fix up a place for her 'longside o' you an' Dinah.' She was de old cook.

"'Come 'long,' I says, 'Miss Nannie,' an' I dropped a curtsey same 's if she was a princess. An' so she was, an' Marse Henry's own eyes in her head, an' 'nough like him to be his own chile. 'I 'll hab ev'ything ready for ye,' I says. 'You wait here an' take de air,' an' I got a chair an' sot her down on de po'ch, an' ole Sam brung her some cake, an' I went to git de room ready — de room offn de kitchen pantry, where dey puts de overseer's chillen when dey come to see him.

"Purty soon Miss Rachel come down an' went up an' kissed her — dat is, Sam said so, though I ain't never seen her kiss her dat time nor no other time. Miss Rachel an' de mist'ess was bofe split out o' de same piece o' kindlin', an' what one was agin t' other was agin — a blind man could see dat. Miss Rachel never liked Miss Nannie from de fust, she was dat cross-grained and pernicketty. No matter what Miss Nannie done to please her it warn't good 'nough for her. Why, do you know, when de other chillen come over from de nex' plantation Miss Rachel would n't send for Miss Nannie to come in de parlor. No, suh, dat she would n't! An' dey 'd run off an' leave her, too, when dey was gwine picknickin', an' treat dat chile owdacious, sayin' she was po' white trash, an' charity chile, an' things like dat, till I would go an' tell Marse Henry 'bout it. Den dere would be a 'ruction, an' Marse Henry 'd blaze out, an' jes 's soon 's he was off agin to Frankfort — an' he was dere mos' of de time, for he was one o' dese yere ole-timers dat dey could n't git 'long widout at de Legislater — dey 'd treat her wus 'n ever. Soon 's Dinah an' me see dat, we kep' Miss Nannie 'long wid us much as we could. She 'd eat wid 'em when dere warn't no company 'round, but dat was 'bout all."

"Did they send her to school?" I asked, fearing she would again lose the thread. My picture had a new meaning for me now that it looked like her heroine.

"No, suh, dat dey did n't, 'cept to de schoolhouse at de cross-roads whar eve'y-body's chillen went. But dey sent Miss Rachel to a real highty-tighty school, dat dey did, down to Louisville. Two winters she was dere, an' eve'y time when she come home for holiday times she had mo' airs dan when she went away. Marse Henry wanted bofe chillen to go, but dat woman outdid him, an' she faced him up an' down dat dere warn't money 'nough for two, an' dat her daughter was de fittenest, an' all dat, an' he give in. I did n't hear it, but ole Sam did, an' his han' shook so he mos' spilt de soup. But law, honey, dat did n't make no diff'ence to Miss Nannie. She 'd go off by herse'f wid her books an' sit all day under de trees, an' sing to herse'f jes' like a bird, an' dey 'd sing to her, an' all dat time her face was a-beamin' an' her hair shinin' like gold, an' she a-growin' taller, an' her eyes gittin' bigger an' bigger, an' brighter, an' her little footses white an' cunnin' as a rabbit's.

" De only place whar she did go outside de big house was over to Mis' Morgan's, who lived on de nex' plantation. Miss Morgan did n't hab no chillen of her own, an' she 'd send for Miss Nannie to come an' keep her company, she was dat dead lonesome, an' dey was glad 'nough to let dat chile go so dey could git her out o' de house. Ole Sam allers said dat, for he heared 'em talk at table an' knowed what was gwine on.

" Purty soon long come de time when Miss Rachel done finish her eddication, an' she come back to de big house an' sot herse'f up to 'ceive company. She warn't bad lookin' in dem days, I mus' say, an' if dat woman's sperit had n't 'a' been in her she might 'a' pulled through. But dere warn't no fotch-ing up could stand agin dat blood. Miss Rachel 'd git dat ornery dat you could n't do nuffin wid her, jes' like her maw. De fust real out-an'-out beau she had was Dr. Tom Boling. He lived 'bout fo'teen miles out o' Lexin'ton on de big plantation, an' was de richest young man in our parts. His paw had died 'bout two years befo' an' lef' him mo' money dan he could th'ow away, an' he 'd jes' come back from Philadelphy, whar he 'd been a-learnin' to be a doctor. He met Miss Rachel at a party in Louisville, an' de fust Sunday she come home he driv over to see her. If ye could 'a' seen de mist'ess when she see him comin' in de gate! All in his ridin' boots an' his yaller breeches an' bottle-green coat, an' his servant a-ridin' behind to hold de horses.

"Ole Sam an' me was a-watchin' de mist'ess peekin' th'ough de blind at him, her eyes a-blazin', an' Sam laughed so he had to stuff a napkin in his mouf to keep 'er from hearin' him. Well, suh, dat went on all de summer. Eve'y time he come de mist'ess 'd be dat sweet mos' make a body sick to see her, an' when he 'd stay away she was dat pesky dere warn't no livin' wid her. Of co'se dere was plenty mo' gemmen co'rting Miss Rachel, too, but none o' dem did n't count wid de mist'ess 'cept de doctor, 'cause he was rich, dat 's all dere was to 't, 'cause he was rich. I tell ye ole Sam had to tell many a lie to the other gemmen, sayin' Miss Rachel was sick or somethin' else when she was a-waitin' for de doctor to come, and was feared he might meet some of 'em an' git skeered away.

"Miss Nannie, she 'd watch him, too, from behind de kitchen door, or scrunched down lookin' over de pantry winder sill, an' den she 'd tell Dinah an' me what he did, an' how he got off his horse an' han' de reins to de boy, an' slap his boots wid his ridin' whip, like he was a-dustin' off a fly. An' she 'd act it all out for me an' Dinah, an' slap her own frock, an' den she 'd laugh fit to kill herse'f an' dance all 'round de kitchen. Would yo' believe it? No! dere ain't nobody 'd believe it. Dey never asked her to come in once while he was in de parlor, an' dey never once tole him dat Miss Nannie was a-livin' on de top side o' de yearth!

"'Co'se people 'gin to talk, an' ev'ybody said dat Dr. Boling was gittin' nighest de coon, an' dat fust thing dey 'd know dere would be a weddin' in de Gordon fambly. An' den agin dere was plenty mo' people said he was only passin' de time wid Miss

Rachel, an' dat he come to see Marse Henry to talk pol'tics.

"Well, one day, suh, I was a-standin' in de door an' I see him come in a-foot, widout his horse an' servant, an' step up on de po'ch quick an' rap at de do', like he say to himse'f, 'Lemme in; I 'm in a hurry; I got somethin' on my mind.' Ole Sam was jes' a-gwine to open de do' for him when Miss Nannie come a-runnin' in de kitchen from de yard, her cheeks like de roses, her hair a-flyin', an' her big hat hangin' to a string down her back. I gin Sam one look an' he stopped, an' I says to Miss Nannie, 'Run, honey,' I says, 'an' open de do' for ole Sam; I spec',' I says, 'it 's one o' dem peddlers.'

"If you could 'a' seen dat chile's face when she come back!"

Aunt Chloe's hands were now waving above her head, her mouth wide open in her merriment, every tooth shining.

"She was white one minute an' red as a beet de nex'. 'Oh, Aunt Chloe, what did you let me go for?' she says. 'Oh! I would n't 'a' let him see me like dis for anythin' in de wo'ld. Oh, I 'm dat put out.'

"'What did he say to ye, honey?' I says.

"'He did n't say nuffin; he jes' look at me an' say he beg my pardon, an' was Miss

Rachel in, an' den I said I'd run an' tell her, an' when I come downstairs agin he was a-standin' in de hall wid his eyes up de staircase, an' he never stopped lookin' at me till I come down.'

"'Well, dat won't do you no harm, chile,' I says; 'a cat kin look at a king.'

"Ole Sam was a-watchin' her, too, an' when she'd gone in her leetle room an' shet de do' Sam says, 'I'll lay if Marse Tom Boling had anythin' on his mind when he come here to-day it's mighty onsettled by dis time.'

"Nex' time Dr. Tom Boling come he say to de mist'ess, 'Who's dat young lady,' he says, 'dat opened de door for me las' time I was here? I hoped to see her agin. Is she in?'

"Den dey bofe cooked up some lie 'bout her bein' over to Mis' Morgan's or somethin', an' as soon's he was gone dey come down an' riz Sam for not 'tendin' de door an' lettin' dat ragged fly-away gal open it. Den dey went for Miss Nannie till dey made her cry, an' she come to me, an' I took her in my lap an' comfo'ted her like I allers did.

"De nex' time he come he says, 'I hear dat yo'r niece, Miss Nannie Barnes, is livin' wid you, an' dat she is ve'y 'sclusive. I hope dat you'll 'suade her to come in de parlor,' he says. Dem was his ve'y words. Sam was a-standin' close to him as I am to you an' he heared him.

"'She ain't yet in s'ciety,' de mist'ess says, 'an' she 's dat wild dat we can't p'esent her.'

"'Oh! is dat so?' he says. 'Is she in now?'

"'No,' she says, 'she 's over to Mis' Morgan's.'

"Dat was a fac' dis time; she 'd gone dat very mawnin'. Den Miss Rachel come down, an' co'se Sam did n't hear no mo' 'cause he had to go out. Purty soon out de Doctor come. Dese visits, min' ye, was gittin' shorter an' shorter, though he do come as often, an' over he goes to Mis' Morgan's hisse'f.

"Now I doan' know what he said to Miss Nannie, or what passed 'twixt 'em, 'cause she did n't tell me. Only dat she said he had come to see Mis' Morgan 'bout some land matters, an' dat Mis' Morgan interjuced 'em, but nuffin mo'. Lord bless dat chile! An', suh, dat was de fust time she ever kep' anythin' from her ole mammy. Dat made me mo' glad 'n ever. I knowed den dey was bofe hit.

"But my lan', de fur begin to fly when de mist'ess an' Miss Rachel heared 'bout dat visit!

"'What you mean by makin' eyes at Dr. Boling? Don't you know he's good as 'gaged to my daughter?' de mist'ess said. Dat was a lie, for he never said a word to Miss Rachel; ole Sam could tole you dat. 'Git out o' my house, you good-for-nothin' pauper, an' take yo' rags wid ye.'

"I see right away de fat was in de fire. Marse Henry warn't spected home till de nex' Sunday, an' so I tuk her over to Mis' Morgan, an' den I ups an' tells her eve'ything dat woman had done to dat chile since de day she come. An' when I'd done she tuk Miss Nannie by de han' an' she says: —

"'You won't never want a home, chile, so long as I live. Go back, Chloe, an' git her clo'es.' But I did n't git 'em. I knowed Marse Henry 'd raise de roof when he come, an' he did, bless yo' heart. Went over his-se'f an' got her, an' brought her home, an' dat night when Dr. Boling come he made her sit down in de parlor, an' 'fo' he went home dat night de Doctor he say to Marse Henry, 'I want yo' permission, Mister Gordon, to pay my addresses to Miss Nannie, yo' niece.' Sam was a-standing close as he could git to de door, an' he heard ev'y word. Now he ain't never said dat, mind ye, to Marse Henry 'bout Miss Rachel! An' dat's why I know dat he warn't hit unto death wid her.

"Well, do you know, suh, dat dat woman was dat owdacious she would n't let 'em see each other after dat 'cept on de front po'ch. Would n't let 'em come in de house; make 'em do all dere co'rtin' on de steps an' out at de paster gate. De doctor would rare an' pitch an' git white in de face at de scand'lous way dat Miss Barnes was bein' treated, until Miss Nannie put bofe her leetle han's on his'n, soothin' like, an' den he 'd grab 'em an' kiss 'em like he 'd eat 'em up. Sam cotched him at it, an' done tole me; an' den dey 'd sa'nter off down de po'ch, sayin' it was too hot or too cool, or dat dey was lookin' for birds' nests in de po'ch vines, till dey 'd git to de far end, where de mist'ess nor Sam nor nobody else could n't hear what dey was a-sayin' an' a-whisperin', an' dere dey 'd sit fer hours.

"But I tell ye de doctor had a hard time a-gittin' her even when Marse Henry gin his consent. An' he never would 'a' got her if Miss Rachel, jes' for spite, I spec', had n't 'a' took up wid Colonel Todhunter's son dat was a-co'rtin' on her too, an' run off an' married him. Den Miss Nannie knowed she was free to follow her own heart.

"I tell you it 'd 'a' made ye cry yo' eyes out, suh, to see dat chile try an' fix herse'f up to meet him de days an' nights she knowed he was comin', an' she wid jes' one white frock to her name. An' we all felt jes' as bad as her. Dinah would wash it an' I 'd smooth her hair, an' ole Sam 'd git her a fresh rose to put in her neck.

"Purty soon de weddin' day was 'pinted, an' me an' Dinah an' ole Sam gin to wonder how dat chile was a-gwine to git clo'es to be married in. Sam heared ole marster ask dat same question at de table, an' he see him gib de mist'ess de money to buy 'em for her, an' de mist'ess said dat she reckoned 'Miss Nannie's people would want de priv'lege o' dressin' her now dat she was a-gwine to marry dat wo'thless young doctor, Tom Boling, dat nobody would n't hab in de house, but dat if dey did n't she 'd gin her some of Miss Rachel's clo'es, an' if dem warn't 'nough den she 'd spen' de money to de best advantage.' Dem was her ve'y words. Sam heared her say 'em. I knowed dat meant dat de chile would go naked, for she would n't a-worn none o' Miss Rachel's rubbish, an' not a cent would she git o' de money. So I got dat ole white frock out, an' Dinah found a white ribbon in a ole trunk in de garret, an' washed an' ironed it to tie 'round her waist, an' Miss Nannie come an' look at it, an' when she see it de tears riz up in her eyes.

"'Doan' you cry, chile,' I says. 'He ain't lovin' ye for yo' clo'es, an' never did. Fust time he see ye yo' was purty nigh barefoot. It 's you he wants, not yo' frocks, honey;' an' den de sun come out in her face an' her eyes dried up, an' she gin to smile an' sing like a robin after de rain.

"Purty soon 'long come Chris'mas time, an' me an' ole Sam an' Dinah was a-watchin' out to see what Marse Tom Boling was gwine to gin his bride, fur she was purty nigh dat, as dey was to be married de week after Chris'-mas. Well, suh, de mawnin' 'fore Chris'mas come, an' den de arternoon come, an' den de night come, an' mos' ev'y hour somebody sent somethin' for Miss Rachel, an' yet not one scrap of nuffin big as a chink-a-pin come for Miss Nannie. Dinah an' me was dat onres'-less dat we could n't sleep. Miss Nannie did n't say nuffin when she went to bed, but I see a little shadder creep over her face an' I knowed right away what hurted her.

"Well, de nex' mawnin' — Chris'mas mawn-in' dat was — ole Sam come a-bustin' in de kitchen do', a-hollerin' loud as he could hol-ler" — Aunt Chloe was now rocking herself back and forth, clapping her hands as she talked — "dat dere was a trunk on de front po'ch for Miss Nannie dat was dat heavy it tuk fo' niggers to lif' it. I run, an' Dinah run, an' when we got to de trunk mos' all de niggers was thick 'round it as flies, an' Miss Nannie was standin' over it readin' a card wid her name on it an' a 'scription sayin' dat it was 'a Chris'mas gif', wid de compliments of a friend.' But who dat friend was, whether it was Marse Henry, who sent it dat way so dat woman would n't tear his hair out; or whether Mis' Morgan sent it, dat had n't mo'n 'nough money to live on; or whether some of her own kin in Indiany, dat was dirt po', stole de money an' sent it; or whether de young Dr. Tom Boling, who had mo' money dan all de banks in Lexin'ton, done did it, don't nobody know till dis day, 'cept me an' ole Sam, an' we ain't tellin'.

"But, my soul alive, de insides of dat trunk took de bref clean out o' de mist'ess an' Miss Rachel. Sam opened it, an' I tuk out de things. Honey! dere was a weddin' dress all white satin dat would stand alone, — jes' de ve'y mate of de one you got in dat picter 'fore ye, — an' a change'ble silk, dat heavy! an' a plaid one, an' eve'ything a young lady could git on her back from her skin out, an' a thousand-dollar watch an' chain. I wore dat watch myse'f; Miss Nannie was standin' by me, a-clappin' her han's an' laughin', an' when dat watch an' chain came out she jes' th'owed de chain over my neck an' stuck de leetle watch in my bosom, an' says, 'Dere, you dear ole mammy, go look at you'se'f in de glass an' see how fine you is.'

"De nex' week come de weddin'. I'll never forgit dat weddin' to my dyin' day. Marse Tom Boling driv in wid a coach an' four an' two outriders, an' de horses wore white ribbons on dere ears; an' de coachman had flowers in his coat mos' big as his head, an' dey whirled up in front of de po'ch, an' out he stepped in his blue coat an' brass buttons an' a yaller wais'coat,—yaller as a gourd,—an' his bell-crown hat in his han'. She was a-waitin' for him wid dat white satin dress on, an' de chain 'round her neck, an' her lil footses tied up wid silk ribbons de ve'y match o' dem you got pictered, an' her face shinin' like a angel. An' all de niggers was a-standin' 'roun' de po'ch, dere eyes out'n dere heads, an' Marse Henry was dere in his new clo'es lookin' so grand, an' Sam in his white gloves, an' me in a new head han'chief.

"Eve'ybody was happy 'cept one. Dat one was de mist'ess, standin' in de door. She would n't come out to de coach where de horses was a-champin' de bits an' de froth a-droppin' on de groun', an' she would n't speak to Marse Tom. She kep' back in de do'way.

"Miss Rachel was dat mean she would n't come downstairs.

"Miss Nannie gib Marse Tom Boling her han' an' look up in his face like a queen, an' den she kissed Marse Henry, an' whispered somethin' in his ear dat nobody did n't hear, only de tears gin to jump out an' roll down his cheeks, an' den she looked de mist'ess full in de face, an' 'thout a word dropped her a low curtsey.

"I come de las'. She looked at me for a minute wid her eyes a-swimmin', an' den she th'owed her arms roun' my neck an' hugged an' kissed me, an' den I see an arm slip 'roun' her wais' an' lif' her in de coach. Den de horses gin a plunge an' dey was off.

"An' arter dat dey had five years — de happiest years dem two ever seen. I know, 'cause Marse Henry gin me to her, an' I lived wid 'em day in an' day out till dat baby come, an' den" —

Aunt Chloe stopped and reached out her hand as if to steady herself. The tears were streaming down her cheeks.

Then she advanced a step, fixed her eyes on the portrait, and in a voice broken with emotion, said : —

"Honey, chile, — honey, chile, — is you tired a-waitin' for yo' ole mammy? Keep a-watchin', honey — keep a-watchin' — It won't be long now 'fore I come. Keep a-watchin'."

A WATERLOGGED TOWN

HE was backed up against the Column of the Lion, holding at bay a horde of gondoliers who were shrieking, "Gondola! Gondola!" as only Venetian gondoliers can. He had a half-defiant look, like a cornered stag, as he stood there protecting a small wizen-faced woman of an uncertain age, dressed in a long gray silk duster and pigeon-winged hat — one of those hats that looked as if the pigeon had alighted on it and exploded.

"No, durn ye, I don't want no gon-*do*-la; I got one somewhere round here if I can find it."

If his tall gaunt frame, black chin whisker, and clearly defined features had not located him instantly in my mind, his dialect would have done so.

"You 'll probably find your gondola at the next landing," I said, pointing to the steps.

He looked at me kindly, took the woman by the arm, as if she had been under arrest, and marched her to the spot indicated.

In another moment I felt a touch on my shoulder. "Neighbor, ain't you from the U. S. A.?"

I nodded my head.

"Shake! It 's God's own land!" and he disappeared in the throng.

The next morning I was taking my coffee in the café at the Britannia, when I caught a pair of black eyes peering over a cup, at a table opposite. Then six feet and an inch or two of raw untilled American rose in the air, picked up his plates, cup, and saucer, and, crossing the room, hooked out a chair with his left foot from my table, and sat down.

"You 're the painter feller that helped me out of a hole yesterday? Yes, I knowed it; I see you come in to dinner last night. Eliz-a-beth said it was you, but you was so almighty rigged up in that swallow-tailed coat of yourn I did n't catch on for a minute, but Eliza-beth said she was dead sure."

"The lady with you — your wife?"

"Not to any alarming extent, young man. Never had one — she 's my sister — only one I got; and this summer she took it into her head — you don't mind my setting here, do you? I 'm so durned lonesome among these jabbering Greeks I 'm nearly froze stiff. Thank ye! — took it into her head she'd come over here, and of course I had to bring her. You ain't never traveled around, perhaps, with a young girl of fifty-five, with her head crammed full of hifalutin' notions, — convents

"HER HEAD CRAMMED FULL OF HIFALUTIN' NOTIONS"

and early masters and Mont Blancs and Bon Marchés, — with just enough French to make a muddle of everything she wants to get. Well, that 's Eliza-beth. First it was a circulating library, at Unionville, back of Troy, where I live; then come a course of lectures twice a week on old Edinburgh and the Alps and German cities; and then, to cap all, there come a cuss with magic-lantern slides of 'most every old ruin in Europe, and half our women were crazy to get away from home, and Elizabeth worse than any of 'em; and so I got a couple of Cook's tickets out and back, and here we are; and I don't mind saying," and a wicked, vindictive look filled his eyes, "that of all the cussed holes I ever got into in my life, this here Venice takes — the — cake. Here, John Henry, bring me another cup of coffee; this 's stone-cold. P. D. Q., now! Don't let me have to build a fire under you." This to a waiter speaking every language but English.

"Do not the palaces interest you?" I asked inquiringly, in my effort to broaden his views.

"Palaces be durned! Excuse my French. Palaces! A lot of caved-in old rookeries; with everybody living on the second floor because the first one 's so damp ye 'd get your die-and-never-get-over-it if you lived in the basement, and the top floors so leaky that you go to bed under an umbrella; and they all braced up with iron clamps to keep 'em from falling into the canal, and not a square inch on any one of 'em clean enough to dry a shirt on! What kind of holes are they for decent — Now see here," laying his hand confidingly on my shoulder, "just answer me one question — you seem like a level-headed young man, and ought to give it to me straight. Been here all summer, ain't you?"

"Yes."

"Been coming years, ain't you?"

I nodded my head.

"Well, now, I want it straight," — and he lowered his voice, — "what does a sensible man find in an old waterlogged town like this?"

I gave him the customary answer: the glories of her past; the picturesque life of the lagoons; the beauty of her palaces, churches, and gardens; the luxurious gondolas, etc., etc.

"Don't see it," he broke out before I had half finished. "As for the gon-do-las, you're dead right, and no mistake. First time I settled on one of them cushions I felt just as if I'd settled in a basket of kittens; but as for palaces! Why, the State House at Al-ba-ny knocks 'em cold; and as for gardens! Lord! when I think of mine at home all chock-full of hollyhocks and sunflowers and morning-glories, and then think what a first-class cast-iron idiot I am wandering around here" — He gazed abstractedly at the ceiling for a moment as if the thought overpowered him, and then went on, "I 've got a stock-farm six miles from Unionville, where I 've got some three-year-olds can trot in 2.23 — Gardens!" — suddenly remembering his first train of thought, — "they simply ain't in it. And as for ler-goons! We 've got a river sailing along in front of Troy that may n't be so wide, but it 's a durned sight safer and longer, and there ain't a gallon of water in it that ain't as sweet as a daisy; and that 's what you can't say of these streaks of mud around here, that smell like a dumping-ground." Here he rose from his chair, his voice filling the room, the words dropping slowly: "I — ain't — got — no — use — for — a — place — where — there — ain't — a — horse — in — the — town, — and every — cellar — is — half — full — of — water."

A few mornings after, I was stepping into my gondola when I caught sight of the man from Troy sitting in a gondola surrounded by his trunks. His face expressed supreme content, illumined by a sort of grim humor, as if some master effort of his life had been rewarded with more than usual success. Eliz-a-beth was tucked away on "the basket of kittens," half hidden by the linen curtains.

"Off?" I said inquiringly.

"You bet!"

"Which way?"

"Paris, and then a bee-line for New York."

"But you are an hour too early for your train."

He held his finger to his lips and knitted his eyebrows.

"What 's that?" came a shrill plaintive voice from the curtains. "An hour more? George, please ask the gentleman to tell the gondolier to take us to Salviate's; we 've got time for that glass mirror, and I can't bear to leave Venice without"—

"Eliza-beth, you sit where you air, if it takes a week. No Salviate's in mine, and no glass mirror. We are stuffed now so jammed full of wooden goats, glass bottles, copper buckets, and old church rags that I had to jump on my trunk to lock it." Then waving his hand to me, he called out as I floated off, "This craft is pointed for home, and don't you forget it."

THE BOY IN THE CLOTH CAP

I HAD seen the little fellow but a moment before, standing on the car platform and peering wistfully into the night, as if seeking some face in the hurrying crowd at the station. I remembered distinctly the cloth cap pulled down over his ears, his chubby, rosy cheeks, and the small baby hand clutching the iron rail of the car, as I pushed by and sprang into a hack.

"Lively, now, cabby; I have n't a minute," and I handed my driver a trunk check.

Outside the snow whirled and eddied, the drifts glistening white in the glare of the electric light.

I drew my fur coat closer around my throat, and beat an impatient tattoo with my feet. The storm had delayed the train, and I had less than an hour in which to dine, dress, and reach my audience.

Two minutes later something struck the cab with a force that rattled every spoke in the wheels. It was my trunk, and cabby's head, white with snow, was thrust through the window.

"Morgan House, did you say, boss?"

"Yes, and on the double-quick."

Another voice now sifted in — a small, thin, pleading voice, too low and indistinct for me to catch the words from where I sat.

"Want to go where?" cried cabby. The conversation was like one over the telephone, in which only one side is heard. "To the orphan asylum? Why, that's three miles from here. . . . Walk? . . . See, here, sonny, you would n't get halfway. . . . No, I can't take yer — got a load."

My own head had filled the window now.

"Here, cabby, don't stand there all night! What's the matter, anyway?"

"It's a boy, boss, about a foot high, wants to walk to the orphan 'sylum."

"Pass him in."

He did, literally, through the window, without opening the door, his little wet shoes first, then his sturdy legs in wool stockings, round body encased in a pea-jacket, and last, his head, covered by the same cloth cap I had seen on the platform. I caught him, feet first, and helped land him on the front seat, where he sat looking at me with staring eyes that shone all the brighter in the glare of the arc light. Next a collar-box and a small paper bundle were handed in. These the little fellow clutched eagerly, one in each hand, his eyes still looking into mine.

"Are you an orphan?" I asked—a wholly thoughtless question, of course.

"Yes, sir."

"Got no father nor mother?"

Another, equally idiotic; but my interest in the boy had been inspired by the idea of the saving of valuable minutes. As long as he stood outside in the snow, he was an obstruction. Once aboard, I could take my time in solving his difficulties.

"Got a father, sir, but my mother 's dead."

We were now whirling up the street, the cab lighting up and growing pitch dark by turns, depending on the location of the street lamps.

"Where 's your father?"

"Went away, sir." He spoke the words without the slightest change in his voice, neither abashed nor too bold, but with a simple straightforwardness which convinced me of their truth.

"Do you want to go to the asylum?"

"Yes, sir."

"Why?"

"Because I can learn everything there is to learn, and there is n't any other place for me to go."

This was said with equal simplicity. No whining; no "me mother 's dead, sir, an' I ain't had nothin' to eat all day," etc. Not that air about him at all. It was merely the statement of a fact which he felt sure I knew all about.

"What's your name?"

"Ned."

"Ned what?"

"Ned Rankin, sir."

"How old are you?"

"I'm eight" — then, thoughtfully — "no, I'm nine years old."

"Where do you live?"

I was firing these questions one after the other without the slightest interest in either the boy or his welfare. My mind was on my lecture, and the impatient look on the faces of the audience, and the consulted watch of the chairman of the committee, followed by the inevitable: "You are not very prompt, sir," etc. "Our people have been in their seats," etc. If the boy had previously replied to my question as to where he lived, I had forgotten the name of the town.

"I live" — Then he stopped. "I live in — Do you mean now?" he added simply.

"Yes."

There was another pause. "I don't know, sir; maybe they won't let me stay."

Another foolish question. Of course, if he

had left home for good, and was now on his way to the asylum for the first time, his present home was this hack.

But he had won my interest now. His words had come in tones of such directness, and were so calm, and gave so full a statement of the exact facts, that I leaned over quickly, and began studying him a little closer.

I saw that this scrap of a boy wore a gray woolen suit, and I noticed that the cap was made of the same cloth as the jacket, and that both were the work of some inexperienced hand, with uneven, unpressed seams — the seams of a flat-iron, not a tailor's goose. Instinctively my mind went back to what his earlier life had been.

"Have you got any brothers and sisters, my boy?"

"Yes, sir."

"Where are they?"

"I don't know, sir; I was too little to remember."

The pathos of this answer stirred me all the more.

"Who 's been taking care of you ever since your father left you?" I had lowered my voice now to a more confidential tone.

"A German man."

"What did you leave him for?"

"He had no work, and he took me to the priest."

"When?"

"Last week, sir."

"What did the priest do?"

"He gave me these clothes. Don't you think they 're nice? The priest's sister made them for me — all but the stockings; she bought those."

As he said this he lifted his arms so I could look under them, and thrust out toward me his two plump legs. I said the clothes were very nice, and that I thought they fitted him very well, and I felt his chubby knees and calvės as I spoke, and ended by getting hold of his soft wee hand, which I held on to. His fingers closed tightly over mine, and a slight smile lighted up his face. It seemed good to him to have something to hold on to. I began again: —

"Did the priest send you here?"

"Yes, sir. Do you want to see the letter?" The little hand — the free one — fumbled under the jacket, loosened the two lower buttons, and disclosed a white envelope pinned to his shirt.

"I 'm to give it to 'em at the asylum. But I can't unpin it. He told me not to."

"That 's right, my boy. Leave it where it is."

"You poor little rat," I said to myself. "This is pretty rough on you. You ought to be tucked up in some warm bed, not out here alone in this storm."

The boy felt for the pin in the letter, reassured himself that it was safe, and carefully rebuttoned his jacket. I looked out of the window, and caught glimpses of houses flying by, with lights in their windows, and now and then the cheery blaze of a fire. Then I looked into his eyes again. I still had hold of his hand.

"Surely," I said to myself, "this boy must have some one soul who cares for him." I determined to go a little deeper.

"How did you get here, my boy?" I had leaned nearer to him.

"The priest put me on the train, and a lady told me where to get off."

"Oh, a lady!" Now I was getting at it! Then he was not so desolate; a lady had looked after him. "What 's her name?" This with increased eagerness.

"She did n't tell me, sir."

I sank back on my seat. No! I was all wrong. It was a positive, undeniable, piteous fact. Seventy millions of people about him, and not one living soul to look to. Not a tie that connected him with anything. A leaf blown across a field; a bottle adrift in the sea, sailing from no port and bound for no haven. I got hold of his other hand, and looked down into his eyes, and an almost irresistible desire seized me to pick him up in my arms and hug him; he was too big to kiss, and too little to shake hands with; hugging was all there was left. But I did n't. There was something in his face that repelled any such familiarity, — a quiet dignity, pluck, and patience that inspired more respect than tenderness, that would make one want rather to touch his hat to him.

Here the cab stopped with so sudden a jerk that I had to catch him by the arms to steady him. Cabby opened the door.

"Morgan House, boss. Goin 's awful, or I 'd got ye here sooner."

The boy looked up into my face; not with any show of uneasiness, only a calm patience. If he was to walk now, he was ready.

"Cabby, how far is it to the asylum?" I asked.

"'Bout a mile and a half."

"Throw that trunk off and drive on. This boy can't walk."

"I 'll take him, boss."

"No; I 'll take him myself. Lively, now."

I looked at my watch. Twenty minutes of the hour had gone. I would still have time to jump into a dress suit, but the dinner must be brief. There came a seesaw rocking, then a rebound, and a heavy thud told where the trunk had fallen. The cab sped on round a sharp corner, through a narrow street, and across a wide square.

Suddenly a thought rushed over me that culminated in a creeping chill. Where was his trunk? In my anxiety over my own, I had forgotten the boy's.

I turned quickly to the window, and shouted:—

"Cabby! *Cabby*, you did n't leave the boy's trunk, too, did you?"

The little fellow slid down from the seat, and began fumbling around in the dark.

"No, sir; I 've got 'em here;" and he held up the collar box and brown paper bundle!

"Is that all?" I gasped.

"Oh, no, sir! I got ten cents the lady give me. Do you want to see it?" and he began cramming his chubby hand into his side pocket.

"No, my son, I don't want to see it."

I did n't want to see anything in particular. His word was good enough. I could n't, really. My eyelashes somehow had got tangled up in each other, and my pupils would n't work. It 's queer how a man's eyes act sometimes.

We were now reaching the open country. The houses were few and farther apart. The street lamps gave out; so did the telegraph wires festooned with snow loops. Soon a big building, square, gray, sombre-looking, like a jail, loomed up on a hill. Then we entered a gate between flickering lamps, and tugged up a steep road, and stopped. Cabby sprang down and rang a bell, which sounded in the white stillness like a fire-gong. A door opened, and a flood of light streamed out, showing the kindly face and figure of an old priest in silhouette, the yellow glow forming a golden background.

"Come, sonny," said cabby, throwing open the cab door.

The little fellow slid down again from the seat, caught up the box and bundle, and, looking me full in the face, said:—

"It *was* too far to walk."

There were no thanks, no outburst. He was merely a chip in the current. If he had just escaped some sunken rock, it was the way with chips like himself. All boys went to asylums, and had no visible fathers nor invisible mothers nor friends. This talk about boys going swimming, and catching bull-frogs, and robbing birds' nests, and playing ball, and "hooky," and marbles, was all moonshine. Boys never did such things, except in story-books. He was a boy himself, and knew. There could n't anything better happen to a boy than being sent to an orphan asylum. Everybody knew that. There was nothing strange about it. That 's what boys were made for.

All this was in his eyes.

. . . .

When I reached the platform and faced my audience, I was dinnerless, half an hour late, and still in my traveling dress.

I began as follows: —

"Ladies and gentlemen, I ask your forgiveness. I am very sorry to have kept you waiting, but I could not help it. I was occupied in escorting to his suburban home one of your most distinguished citizens."

And I described the boy in the cloth cap, with his box and bundle, and his patient, steady eyes, and plump little legs in the yarn stockings.

I was forgiven.

BETWEEN SHOWERS IN DORT

THERE be inns in Holland — not hotels, not pensions, nor stopping-places — just inns. The Bellevue at Dort is one, and the Holland Arms is another, and the — no, there are no others. Dort only boasts these two, and Dort to me is Holland.

The rivalry between these two inns has been going on for years, and it still continues. The Bellevue, fighting for place, elbowed its way years ago to the water-line, and took its stand on the river-front, where the windows and porticos could overlook the Maas dotted with boats. The Arms, discouraged, shrank back into its corner, and made up in low windows, smoking-rooms, and private bathroom — one for the whole house — what was lacking in porticos and sea view. Then followed a slight skirmish in paint, — red for the Arms and yellow-white for the Bellevue; and a flank movement of shades and curtains, — linen for the Arms and lace for the Bellevue. Scouting parties were next ordered out of porters in caps, banded with silk ribbons, bearing the names of their respective hostelries. Yacob of the Arms

THROUGH STREETS EMBOWERED IN TREES

was to attack weary travelers on alighting from the train, and acquaint them with the delights of the downstairs bath, and the dark-room for the kodakers, all free of charge. And Johan of the Bellevue was to give minute descriptions of the boats landing in front of the dining-room windows and of the superb view of the river.

It is always summer when I arrive in Dordrecht. I don't know what happens in winter, and I don't care. The groundhog knows enough to go into his hole when the snow begins to fly, and to stay there until the sun thaws him out again. Some tourists could profit by following his example.

It is summer then, and the train has rolled into the station at Dordrecht, or beside it, and the traps have been thrown out, and Peter, my boatman — he of the "Red Tub," a craft with an outline like a Dutch vrou, quite as much beam as length (we go a-sketching in this boat) — Peter, I say, who has come to the train to meet me, has swung my belongings over his shoulder, and Johan, the porter of the Bellevue, with a triumphant glance at Yacob of the Arms, has stowed the trunk on the rear platform of the street tram, — no cabs or trucks, if you please, in this town, — and the one-horse car has jerked its way around short curves and up through streets embowered in trees and paved with cobblestones scrubbed as clean as china plates, and over quaint bridges with glimpses of sluggish canals and queer houses, and so on to my lodgings.

And mine host, Heer Boudier, waiting on the steps, takes me by the hand and says the same room is ready and has been for a week.

Inside these two inns, the only inns in Dort, the same rivalry exists. But my parallels must cease. Mine own inn is the Bellevue, and my old friend of fifteen years, Heer Boudier, is host, and so loyalty compels me to omit mention of any luxuries but those to which I am accustomed in his hostelry.

Its interior has peculiar charms for me. Scrupulously clean, simple in its appointments and equipment, it is comfort itself. Tyne is responsible for its cleanliness — or rather, that particular portion of Tyne which she bares above her elbows. Nobody ever saw such a pair of sledge-hammer arms as Tyne's on any girl outside of Holland. She is eighteen; short, square-built, solid as a Dutch cheese, fresh and rosy as an English milkmaid; moon-faced, mild-eyed as an Alderney heifer, and as strong as a three-year-old. Her back and sides are as straight as a plank; the front side is straight too. The main joint in her body is at the hips. This is so flexible that, wash-cloth in hand, she can lean over the floor without bending her knees and scrub every board in it till it shines like a Sunday dresser. She wears a snow-white cap as dainty as the finest lady's in the land; an apron that never seems to lose the crease of the iron, and a blue print dress bunched up behind to keep it from the slop. Her sturdy little legs are covered by gray yarn stockings which she knits herself; the feet thrust into wooden sabots. These clatter over the cobbles as she scurries about with a crab-like movement, sousing, dousing, and scrubbing as she goes; for Tyne attacks the sidewalk outside with as much gusto as she does the hall and floors.

Johan the porter moves the chairs out of Tyne's way when she begins work, and, lately, I have caught him lifting her bucket up the front steps — a wholly unnecessary proceeding when Tyne's muscular developments are considered. Johan and I had a confidential talk one night, when he brought the mail to my room, — the room on the second floor overlooking the Maas, — in which certain personal statements were made.

When I spoke to Tyne about them the next day, she looked at me with her big blue eyes, and then broke into a laugh, opening her mouth so wide that every tooth in her head flashed white (they always reminded me somehow of peeled almonds). With a little bridling twist of her head she answered that — but, of course, this was a strictly confidential communication, and of so entirely private a nature that no gentleman under the circumstances would permit a single word of it to —

Johan is taller than Tyne, but not so thick through. When he meets you at the station, with his cap and band in his hand, his red hair trimmed behind as square as the end of a whisk-broom, his thin, parenthesis legs and Vienna guardsman waist, — each detail the very opposite, you will note, from Tyne's, — you recall immediately one of George Boughton's typical Dutchmen. The only thing lacking is his pipe; he is too busy for that.

When he dons his dress suit for dinner, and bending over your shoulder asks, in his best English: "Mynheer, don't it now de feesh you haf?" you lose sight of Boughton's Dutchman and see only the cosmopolitan. The transformation is due entirely to continental influences — Dort being one of the main highways between London and Paris — influences so strong that even in this water-logged town on the Maas, bonnets are beginning to replace caps, and French shoes sabots.

The guests that Johan serves at this inn of my good friend Boudier are as odd looking as its interior. They line both sides and the two ends of the long table. Stout Germans in horrible clothes, with stouter wives in worse; Dutchmen from up-country in brown coats and green waistcoats; clerks off on a vacation with kodaks and Cook's tickets; bicyclists in knickerbockers; painters, with large kits and small handbags, who talk all the time and to everybody; gray-whiskered, red-faced Englishmen, with absolutely no conversation at all, who prove to be distinguished persons attended by their own valets, and on their way to Aix or the Engadine, now that the salmon-fishing in Norway is over; school teachers from America, just arrived from Antwerp or Rotterdam, or from across the channel by way of Harwich, their first stopping-place really since they left home — one traveling-dress and a black silk in the bag; all the kinds and conditions and sorts of people who seek out precious little places like Dort, either because they are cheap or comfortable, or because they are known to be picturesque.

I sought out Dort years ago because it was untouched by the hurry that makes life miserable, and the shams that make it vulgar, and I go back to it now every year of my life, in spite of other foreign influences.

And there is no real change in fifteen years. Its old trees still nod over the sleepy canals in the same sleepy way they have done, no doubt, for a century. The rooks — the same rooks, they never die — still swoop in and out of the weather-stained arches high up in the great tower of the Groote Kerk, the old twelfth-century church, the tallest in all Holland; the big-waisted Dutch luggers with rudders painted arsenic green — what would painters do without this green? — doze under the trees, their mooring lines tied to the trunks; the girls and boys, with arms locked, a dozen together, clatter over the cobbles, singing as they walk; the steamboats land and hurry on — "Fop Smit's boats" the signs read — it is pretty close, but I am not part owner in the line; the gossips lean in the doorways or under the windows banked with geraniums and nasturtiums; the cumbersome state carriages with the big ungainly

THE GOSSIPS LEAN IN THE DOORWAYS

horses with untrimmed manes and tails — there are only five of these carriages in all Dordrecht — wait in front of the great houses eighty feet wide and four stories high, some dating as far back as 1512, and still occupied by descendants of the same families; the old women in ivory black, with dabs of Chinese white for sabots and caps, push the same carts loaded with Hooker's green vegetables from door to door; the town crier rings his bell; the watchman calls the hour.

Over all bends the ever-changing sky, one hour close-drawn, gray-lined with slanting slashes of blinding rain, the next piled high with great domes of silver-white clouds inlaid with turquoise blue or hemmed in by low-lying ranges of purple peaks capped with gold.

. . . .

I confess that an acute sense of disappointment came over me when I first saw these gray canals, rain-varnished streets, and rows of green trees. I recognized at a glance that it was not my Holland; not the Holland of my dreams; not the Holland of Mesdag nor Poggenbeck nor Kever. It was a fresher, sweeter, more wholesome land, and with a more breathable air. These Dutch painters had taught me to look for dull, dirty skies, soggy wharves, and dismal perspectives of endless dikes. They had shown me countless windmills, scattered along stretches of wind-swept moors backed by lowering skies, cold gray streets, quaint, leanover houses, and smudgy, grimy interiors. They had enveloped all this in the stifling, murky atmosphere of a western city slowly strangling in clouds of coal smoke.

These Dutch artists were, perhaps, not alone in this falsification. It is one of the peculiarities of modern art that many of its masters cater to the taste of a public who want something that *is not* in preference to something that *is*. Ziem, for instance, had, up to the time of my enlightenment, taught me to love an equally untrue and impossible Venice — a Venice all red and yellow and deep ultra-marine blue — a Venice of unbuildable palaces and blazing red walls.

I do not care to say so aloud, where I can be heard over the way, but if you will please come inside my quarters, and shut the door and putty up the keyhole, and draw down the blinds, I will whisper in your ear that my own private opinion is that even Turner himself would have been an infinitely greater artist had he built his pictures on Venice instead of building them on Turner. I will also be courageous enough to assert that the beauty and dignity of Venetian architecture—an architecture which has delighted many appreciative souls for centuries—finds no place in his canvases, either in detail or in mass. The details may be unimportant, for the soft vapor of the lagoons ofttimes conceals them, but the correct outline of the mass—that is, for instance, the true proportion of the dome of the Salute, that incomparable, incandescent pearl, or the vertical line of the Campanile compared to the roofs of the connecting palaces—should never be ignored, for they are as much a part of Venice, the part that makes for beauty, as the shimmering light of the morning or the glory of its sunsets. So it is that when most of us for the first time reach the water-gates of Venice, the most beautiful of all cities by the sea, we feel a certain shock and must begin to fall in love with a new sweetheart.

So with many painters of the Holland school—not the old Dutch school of landscape painters, but the more modern group of men who paint their native skies with zinc-white toned with London fog, or mummy dust and bitumen. It is all very artistic and full of "tone," but it is not Holland.

There is Clays, for instance. Of all modern painters Clays has charmed and wooed us best with certain phases of Holland life, particularly the burly brown boats lying at anchor, their red and white sails reflected in the water. I love these boats of Clays. They are superbly drawn, strong in color, and admirably painted; the water treatment, too, is beyond criticism. But where are they in Holland? I know Holland from the Zuyder Zee to Rotterdam, but I have never yet seen one of Clays's boats in the original wood.

Thus by reason of such smeary, up and down fairy tales in paint have we gradually become convinced that vague trees, and black houses with staring patches of whitewash, and Vandyke brown roofs are thoroughly characteristic of Holland, and that the blessed sun never shines in this land of sabots.

But does n't it rain? Yes, about half the time, perhaps three quarters of the time. Well, now that I think of it, about all the time. But not continuously; only in intermittent downpours, floods, gushes of water — not once a day but every half hour. Then comes the quick drawing of a gray curtain from a wide expanse of blue, framing ranges of snow-capped cumuli; streets swimming in great pools; drenched leaves quivering in dazzling sunlight, and millions of raindrops flashing like diamonds.

II

BUT Peter, my boatman, cap in hand, is waiting on the cobbles outside the inn door. He has served me these many years. He is a wiry, thin, pinch-faced Dutchman, of perhaps sixty, who spent his early life at sea as man-o'-war's-man, common sailor, and then mate, and his later years at home in Dort, picking up odd jobs of ferriage or stevedoring, or making early gardens. While on duty he wears an old white traveling-cap pulled over his eyes, and a flannel shirt without collar or tie, and sailmaker's trousers. These trousers are caught at his hips by a leather strap supporting a sheath which holds his knife. He cuts everything with this knife, from apples and navy plug to ship's cables and telegraph wire. His clothes are waterproof; they must be, for no matter how hard it rains, Peter is always dry. The water may pour in rivulets from off his cap, and run down his forehead and from the end of his gargoyle of a nose, but no drop ever seems to wet his skin. When it rains the fiercest, I, of course, retreat under the poke-bonnet awning made of cotton duck stretched over barrel hoops that protects the stern of my boat, but Peter never moves. This Dutch rain does not in any way affect him. It is like the Jersey mosquito — it always spares the natives.

Peter speaks two languages, both Dutch. He says that one is English, but he cannot prove it — nobody can. When he opens his mouth you know all about his ridiculous pretensions. He says — "Mynheer, dot manus ist er blowdy rock." He has learned this expression from the English sailors unloading coal at the big docks opposite Pappendrecht, and he has incorporated this much of their slang into his own nut-cracking dialect. He means of course "that man is a bloody rogue." He has a dozen other phrases equally obscure.

Peter's mission this first morning after my arrival is to report that the good ship Red Tub is now lying in the harbor fully equipped for active service. That her aft awning has been hauled taut over its hoops; that her lockers of empty cigar boxes (receptacles for brushes) have been clewed up; the cocoa-matting rolled out the whole length of her

DRENCHED LEAVES QUIVERING

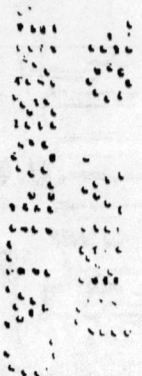

keel, and finally that the water bucket and wooden chair (I use a chair instead of an easel) have been properly stowed.

Before the next raincloud spills over its edges, we must loosen the painter from the iron ring rusted tight in the square stone in the wharf, man the oars, and creep under the little bridge that binds Boudier's landing to the sidewalk over the way, and so set our course for the open Maas. For I am in search of Dutch boats to-day, as near like Clays's as I can find. I round the point above the old India warehouses, I catch sight of the topmasts of two old luggers anchored in midstream, their long red pennants flattened against the gray sky. The wind is fresh from the east, filling the sails of the big windmills blown tight against their whirling arms. The fishing-smacks lean over like dipping gulls; the yellow water of the Maas is flecked with wavy lines of beer foam.

The good ship Red Tub is not adapted to outdoor sketching under these conditions. The poke-bonnet awning acts as a wind-drag that no amount of hard pulling can overcome. So I at once convene the Board of Strategy, Lieutenant-Commander Peter Jansen, Red Tub Navy, in the chair. That distinguished naval expert rises from his water-soaked seat on the cocoa-matting outside the poke bonnet, sweeps his eye around the horizon, and remarks sententiously: —

"It no tam goot day. Blow all dime; we go ba'd-hoose," and he turns the boat toward a low-lying building anchored out from the main shore by huge chains secured to floating buoys.

In some harbors sea-faring men are warned not to "anchor over the water-pipes." In others particular directions are given to avoid "submarine cables planted here." In Dort, where none of these modern conveniences exist, you are notified as follows: "No boats must land at this Bath."

If Peter knew of this rule he said not one word to me as I sat back out of the wet, hived under the poke bonnet, squeezing color-tubes and assorting my brushes. He rowed our craft toward the bath-house with the skill of a man-o'-war's-man, twisted the painter around a short post, and unloaded my paraphernalia on a narrow ledge or plank walk some three feet wide, and which ran around the edge of the floating bath-house.

It never takes me long to get to work, once my subject is selected. I sprang from the boat while Peter handed me the chair, stool, and portfolio containing my stock of gray papers of different tones; opened my sketch frame, caught a sheet of paper tight between its cleats; spread palettes and brushes on the floor at my side; placed the water bucket within reach of my hand, and in five minutes I was absorbed in my sketch.

Immediately the customary thing happened. The big bank of gray cloud that hung over the river split into feathery masses of white framed in blue, and out blazed the glorious sun.

Meantime, Peter had squatted close beside me, sheltered under the lee of the side wall of the bath-house, protected equally from the slant of the driving rain and the glare of the blinding sun. Safe too from the watchful eye of the High Pan-Jam who managed the bath, and who at the moment was entirely oblivious of the fact that only two inches of pine board separated him from an enthusiastic painter working like mad, and an equally alert marine assistant who supplied him with fresh water and charcoal points, both at the moment defying the law of the land, one in ignorance and the other in a spirit of sheer bravado. For Peter must have known the code and the penalty.

The world is an easy place for a painter to

live and breathe in when he is sitting far from the madding crowd — of boys — protected from the wind and sun, watching a sky piled up in mountains of snow, and inhaling ozone that is a tonic to his lungs. When the outline of his sketch is complete and the colors flow and blend, and the heart is on fire; when the bare paper begins to lose itself in purple distances and long stretches of tumbling water, and the pictured boats take definite shape, and the lines of the rigging begin to tell; when little by little, with a pat here and a dab there, there comes from out this flat space a something that thrilled him when he first determined to paint the thing that caught his eye, — not the thing itself, but the spirit, the soul, the feeling, and meaning of the color-poem unrolled before him, — when a painter feels a thrill like this, all the fleets of Spain might bombard him, and his eye would never waver nor his touch hesitate.

I felt it to-day.

Peter did n't. If he had he would have kept still and passed me fresh water and rags and new tubes and whatever I wanted — and I wanted something every minute — instead of disporting himself in an entirely idiotic and disastrous way. Disastrous, because you might have seen the sketch which I began reproduced in these pages had the Lieutenant-Commander, R. T. N., only carried out the orders of the Lord High Admiral commanding the fleet.

A sunbeam began it. It peeped over the edge of the side wall — the wall really was but little higher than Peter's head when he stood erect — and started in to creep down my half-finished sketch. Peter rose in his wrath, reached for my white umbrella, and at once opened it and screwed together the jointed handle. Then he began searching for some convenient supporting hook on which to hang his shield of defence. Next a brilliant, intellectual dynamite-bomb of a thought split his cranium. He would hoist the umbrella *above* the top of the thin wall of the bath-house, resting one half upon its upper edge, drive the iron spike into the plank under our feet, and secure the handle by placing his back against it. No sunbeam should pass him!

The effect can be imagined on the High-Pan-Jam inside the bath-house — an amphibious guardian, oblivious naturally to sun and rain — when his eye fell upon this flag of defiance thrust up above his ramparts. You can imagine, too, the consternation of the peaceful inmates of the open pools, whose laughter had now and then risen above the sough of the wind and splash of the water. Almost immediately I heard the sound of hurrying footsteps from a point where no sound had come before, and there followed the scraping of a pair of toes on the planking behind me, as if some one was drawing himself up.

I looked around and up and saw eight fingers clutching the top of the planking, and a moment later the round face of an astonished Dutchman. I have n't the faintest idea what he said. I did n't know then and I don't know now. I only remember that his dialect sounded like the traditional crackling of thorns under a pot, including the spluttering, and suggesting the equally heated temperature. When his fingers gave out he would drop out of sight, only to rise again and continue the attack.

Here Peter, I must say, did credit to his Dutch ancestors. He did not temporize. He did not argue. He ignored diplomacy at the start, and blazed out that we were out of everybody's way and on the lee side of the structure; that there was no sign up on that side; that I was a most distinguished personage of blameless life and character, and that, rules or no rules, he was going to stay where he was and so was I.

"You tam blowdy rock. It 's s'welve o'clook now — no rule aft' s'welve o'clook, — nopody ba'd now;" — This in Dutch, but it meant that, then turning to me, "You stay — you no go — I brek tam head him." —

None of this interested me. I had heard Peter explode before. I was trying to match the tone of an opalescent cloud inlaid with mother-of-pearl, the shadow side all purplish gray. Its warm high-lights came all right, but I was half out of my head trying to get its shadow-tones true with Payne's gray and cobalt. The cloud itself had already cast its moorings and was fast drifting over the English Channel. It would be out of sight in five minutes.

"Peter — *Peter!*" I cried. "Don't talk so much. Here, give him half a gulden and tell him to dry up. Hand me that sky brush — quick now!"

The High Pan-Jam dropped with a thud to his feet. His swinging footsteps could be heard growing fainter, but no stiver of my silver had lined his pocket.

I worked on. The tea-rose cloud had disappeared entirely; only its poor counterfeit remained. The boats were nearly finished;

another wash over their sails would bring them all right. Then the tramp as of armed men came from the in-shore side of the bath-house. Peter stood up and craned his neck around the edge of the planking, and said in an undertone : —

"Tam b'lice, he come now; nev' mind, you stay 'ere — no go. Tam blowdy rock no mak' you go."

Behind me stood the High Pan-Jam who had scraped his toes on the fence. With him was an officer of police!

Peter was now stamping his feet, swearing in Dutch, English, and polyglot, and threatening to sponge the Dutch government from the face of the universe.

My experience has told me that it is never safe to monkey with a gendarme. He is generally a perfectly cool, self-poised, unimpressionable individual, with no animosity whatever toward you or anybody else, but who intends to be obeyed, not because it pleases him, but because the power behind him compels it. I instantly rose from my stool, touched my hat in respectful military salute, and opened my cigarette-case. The gendarme selected a cigarette with perfect coolness and good humor, and began politely to unfold to me his duties in connection with the municipal laws of Dordrecht. The manager of the bath, he said, had invoked his services. I might not be aware that it was against the law to land on this side of the bath-house, etc.

But the blood of the Jansens was up. Some old Koop or De Witt or Von Somebody was stirring Peter.

"No ba'd aft' s'welve o'clook"—this to me, both fists in the air, one perilously near the officer's face. The original invective was in his native tongue, hurled at Pan-Jam and the officer alike.

"What difference does it make, your Excellency," I asked, "whether I sit in my boat and paint or sit here where there is less motion?"

"None, honored sir," and he took a fresh cigarette (Peter was now interpreting),—"except for the fact that you have taken up your position on the *women's* side of the bath-house. They bathe from twelve o'clock till four. When the ladies saw the umbrella they were greatly disturbed. They are now waiting for you to go away!"

III

MY room at Heer Boudier's commands a full view of the Maas, with all its varied shipping. Its interior fittings are so scrupulously clean that one feels almost uncomfortable lest some of the dainty appointments might be soiled in the using. The bed is the most remarkable of all its comforts. It is more of a box than a bed, and so high at head and foot, and so solid at its sides, that it only needs a lid to make the comparison complete. There is always at its foot an inflated eider-down quilt puffed up like a French soufflé potato; and there are always at its head two little oval pillows solid as bags of ballast, surmounting a bolster that slopes off to an edge. I have never yet found out what this bolster is stuffed with. The bed itself would be bottomless but for the slats. When you first fall overboard into this slough you begin to sink through its layers of feathers, and instinctively throw out your hands, catching at the side boards as a drowning man would clutch at the gunwales of a suddenly capsized boat.

The second night after my arrival, I, in accordance with my annual custom, deposited the contents of this bed in a huge pile outside my door, making a bottom layer of the feathers, then the bolster, and last the soufflé with the hard-boiled eggs on top.

Then I rang for Tyne.

She had forgotten all about the way I liked my sleeping arrangements until she saw the pile of bedding. Then she held her sides with laughter, while the tears streamed down her red cheeks. Of course, the Heer should have a mattress and big English pillows, and no bouncy-bounce, speaking the words not with her lips, but with a gesture of her hand. Then she called Johan to help. I never can see why Tyne always calls Johan to help when there is anything to be done about my room out of the usual order of things,—the sweeping, dusting, etc.,—but she does. I know full well that if she so pleased she could tuck the whole pile of bedding under her chin, pick up the bureau in one hand and the bed in the other, and walk downstairs without even mussing her cap-strings.

When Johan returned with a hair mattress and English pillows,—you can get anything you want at Boudier's,—he asked me if I had heard the news about Peter. Johan, by the way, speaks very good English—for Johan. The Burgomaster, he said, had that day served Peter with a writ. If I had looked out of the window an hour ago, I could have seen the Lieutenant-Commander of the Red Tub, under charge of an officer of the law, on his way to the Town Hall. Peter, he added, had just returned and was at the present moment engaged in scrubbing out the R. T. for active service in the morning.

I at once sent for Peter.

He came up, hat in hand. But there was no sign of weakening. The blood of the Jansens was still in his eye.

"What did they arrest you for, Peter?"

"For make jaw wid de tam bolice. He say I mos' pay two gulden or one tay in jail. Oh, it is notting; I no pay. Dot bolice lie ven he say vimmen ba'd. Nopoty ba'd in de hoose aft' s'welve 'clook."

Later, Heer Boudier tells me that because of Peter's action in resisting the officer in the discharge of his duty, he is under arrest, and that he has but *five days in which to make up his mind* as to whether he will live on bread and water for a day and night in the town jail, or whether he will deplete his slender savings in favor of the state to the extent of two gulden.

"But don't they lock him up, meanwhile?" I asked.

Boudier laughed. "Where would he run to, and for what? To save two gulden?"

My heart was touched. I could not possibly allow Peter to spend five minutes in jail on my account. I should not have slept one wink that night even in my luxurious bed-box with English pillows, knowing that the Lieutenant-Commander was stretched out on a cold floor with a cobblestone under his cheek. I knew, too, how slender was his store, and what a godsend my annual visit had been to his butcher and baker. The Commander of the Red Tub might be impetuous, even aggressive, but by no possible stretch of the imagination could he be considered criminal.

That night I added these two gulden (about eighty cents) to Peter's wages. He thanked me with a pleased twinkle in his eye, and a wrinkling of the leathery skin around his nose and mouth. Then he put on his cap and disappeared up the street.

. . . .

But the inns, quaint canals, and rain-washed streets are not Dort's only distinctions. There is an ancient Groote Kerk, overlaid with colors that are rarely found outside of Holland. It is built of brick, with a huge square tower that rises above the great elms pressing close about it, and which is visible for miles. The moist climate not only encrusts its twelfth-century porch with brown-and-green patches of lichen over the red tones, but dims the great stained-glass windows with films of mould, and covers with streaks of Hooker's green the shadow sides of the long sloping roofs. Even the brick pavements about it are carpeted with strips of green, as fresh in color as if no passing foot had touched them. And few feet ever do touch them, for it is but a small group of worshipers that gather weekly within the old kirk's whitewashed walls.

These faithful few do not find the rich interior of the olden time, for many changes have come over it since its cathedral days, the days of its pomp and circumstance. All its old-time color is gone when you enter its portals, and only staring white walls and rigid, naked columns remain; only dull gray stone floors and hard, stiff-backed benches. I have often sat upon these same benches in the gloom of a fast-fading twilight and looked about me, bemoaning the bareness, and wondering what its *ensemble* must have been in the days of its magnificence. There is nothing left of its glories now but its architectural lines. The walls have been stripped of

AN ANCIENT GROOTE KERK

their costly velvets, tapestries, and banners of silk and gold, the uplifted cross is gone; the haze of swinging censers no longer blurs the vistas, nor the soft light of many tapers illumines their gloom.

I have always believed that duty and beauty should ever go hand in hand in our churches. To me there is nothing too rich in tone, too luxurious in color, too exquisite in line for the House of God. Nothing that the brush of the painter can make glorious, the chisel of the sculptor beautify, or the T-square of the architect ennoble, can ever be out of place in the one building of all others that we dedicate to the Creator of all beauty. I have always thanked Him for his goodness in giving as much thought to the flowers that cover the hillsides as He did to the dull earth that lies beneath; as much care to the matchings of purples and gold in the sunsets as to the blue-black crags that are outlined against them. With these feelings in my heart I have never understood that form of worship which contents itself with a bare barn filled with seats of pine, a square box of a pulpit, a lone pitcher of ice water, and a popular edition of the hymns. But then, I am not a Dutchman.

Besides this town of Dort, filled with

queer warehouses, odd buildings, and cobbled streets, and dominated by this majestic cathedral, there is across the river — just a little way (Peter rows me over in ten minutes) — the Noah's Ark town of Pappendrecht, surrounded by great stretches of green meadow, dotted with black and white cows, and acres and acres of cabbages and garden truck, and tiny farmhouses, and absurdly big barns ; and back of these, and in order to keep all these dry, is a big dike that goes on forever and is lost in the perspective. On both sides of this dike (its top is a road) are built the toy houses facing each other, each one cleaner and better scrubbed than its neighbor, their big windows gay with geraniums.

Farther down is another 'recht — I cannot for the life of me remember the first part of its name — where there is a shipyard and big windlasses and a horse hitched to a sweep, which winds up water-soaked luggers on to rude ways, and great pots of boiling tar, the yellow smoke drifting away toward the sea.

And between these towns of Dort, Pappendrecht, and the other 'recht moves a constant procession of water craft ; a never-ceasing string of low, rakish barges that bear the commerce of Germany out to the sea, each in charge of a powerful tug puffing eagerly in its hurry to reach tide water, besides all the other boats and luggers that sail and steam up and down the forked Maas in front of Boudier's Inn — for Dort is really on an island, the water of the Rhine being divided here. You would never think, were you to watch these ungainly boats, that they could ever arrive anywhere. They look as if they were built to go sideways, endways, or both ways; and yet they mind their helms and dodge in and out and swoop past the long points of land ending in the waving marsh grass, and all with the ease of a steam yacht.

. . . .

These and a hundred other things make me love this quaint old town on the Maas. There is everything within its borders for the painter who loves form and color — boats, queer houses, streets, canals, odd, picturesque interiors, figures, brass milk cans, white-capped girls, and stretches of marsh. If there were not other places on the earth I love equally as well — Venice, for instance — I would be content never to leave its shower-drenched streets. But I know that my gondola, gay in its new *tenta* and polished brasses, is waiting for me in the little canal next the bridge, and I must be off.

Tyne has already packed my trunk, and Johan is ready to take it down the stairs. Tyne sent for him. I did not.

When Johan, like an overloaded burro stumbling down the narrow defile of the staircase, my trunk on his back, disappears through the lower door, Tyne reënters my room, closes the door softly, and tells me that Johan's wages have been raised, and that before I return next summer she and —

But I forgot. This is another strictly confidential communication. Under no possible circumstances could a man of honor — certainly not.

Peter, to my surprise, is not in his customary place when I reach the outer street door. Johan, at my inquiring gesture, grins the width of his face, but has no information to impart regarding Peter's unusual absence.

Heer Boudier is more explicit.

"Where's Peter?" I cry with some impatience.

My host shrugs his shoulders with a helpless movement, and opens wide the fingers of both hands.

"Mynheer, the five days are up. Peter has gone to jail."

"What for?" I ask in astonishment.

"To save two gulden."

ONE OF BOB'S TRAMPS

I HAD passed him coming up the dingy corridor that led to Bob's law office, and knew at once that he was one of Bob's tramps.

When he had squeezed himself through the partly open door and had closed it gently, — closed it with a hand held behind his back, like one who had some favor to ask or some confidence game to play, — he proved to be a man about fifty years of age, fat and short, with a round head partly bald, and hair quite gray. His face had not known a razor for days. He was dressed in dark clothes, once good, showing a white shirt, and he wore a collar without a cravat. Down his cheeks were uneven furrows, beginning at his spilling, watery eyes, and losing themselves in the stubble-covered cheeks, — like old rain-courses dried up, — while on his flat nose were perched a pair of silver-rimmed spectacles, over which he looked at us in a dazed, half-bewildered, half-frightened way. In one hand he held his shapeless slouch hat; the other grasped an old violin wrapped in a grimy red silk handkerchief.

For an instant he stood before the door, bent low with unspoken apologies; then placing his hat on the floor, he fumbled nervously in the breast pocket of his coat, from which he drew a letter, penned in an unknown hand and signed with an unknown name. Bob read it, and passed it to me.

"Please buy this violin," the note ran. "It is a good instrument, and the man needs the money. The price is sixty dollars."

"Who gave you this note?" Bob asked. He never turns a beggar from his door if he can help it. This reputation makes him the target for half the tramps in town.

"Te leader of te orchestra at te theatre. He say he not know you, but dat you loafe good violin. I come von time before, but vas nobody here." Then, after a pause, his wavering eye seeking Bob's, "Blease you buy him?"

"Is it yours?" I asked, anxious to get rid of him. The note trick had been played that winter by half the tramps in town.

"Yes. Mine vor veefteen year," he answered slowly, in an unemotional way.

"Why do you want to sell it?" said Bob, his interest increasing, as he caught the pleading look in the man's eyes.

"I don't vant to sell it — I vant to keep

it; but I haf notting," his hands opening wide. "Ve vas in Phildelphy, ant ten Scranton, ant ten we get here to Peetsburgh, and all te scenery is by te shereef, and te manager haf notting. Vor vourteen tays I valk te streets, virst it is te ofercoat ant vatch, ant yestertay te ledder case vor veefty cents. If you ton't buy him I must keep valking till I come by New York."

"I 've got a good violin," said Bob, softening.

"Ten you don't buy him?" and a look as of a returning pain crossed his hopeless, impassive face. "Vell, I go vay, ten," he said, with a sigh that seemed to empty his heart.

We both looked on in silence as he slowly wrapped the silk rag around it, winding the ends automatically about the bridge and strings, as he had no doubt done a dozen times before that day in his hunt for a customer. Suddenly as he reached the neck he stopped, turned the violin in his hand, and unwound the handkerchief again.

"Tid you oxamine te neck? See how it lays in te hand! Tid you ever see neck like dat? No, you don't see it, never," in a positive tone, looking at us again over the silver rims of his spectacles.

Bob took the violin in his hand. It was evidently an old one and of peculiar shape. The swells and curves of the sides and back were delicately rounded and highly finished. The neck, too, to which the man pointed, was smooth and remarkably graceful, like the stem of an old meerschaum pipe, and as richly colored.

Bob handled it critically, scrutinizing every inch of its surface — he adores a Cremona as some souls do a Madonna — then he walked with it to the window.

"Why, this has been mended!" he exclaimed in surprise and with a trace of anger in his voice. "This is a new neck put on!"

I knew by the tone that Bob was beginning now to see through the game.

"Ah, you vind day oud, do you? Tat *is* a new neck, sure, ant a goot von, put on py Simon Corunden — not Auguste! — Simon! It is better as efer."

I looked for the guileless, innocent expression with the regulation smile that distinguishes most vagabonds on an errand like this, but his lifeless face was unlit by any visible emotion.

Drawing the old red handkerchief from his pocket in a tired, hopeless way, he began twisting it about the violin again.

"Play something on it," said Bob. He evidently believed every word of the impromptu explanation, and was weakening again. Harrowing sighs — chronic for years — or trickling tears shed at the right moment by some grief-stricken woman never failed to deceive him.

"No, I don't blay. I got no heart inside of me to blay," with a weary movement of his hand. He was now tucking the frayed ends of the handkerchief under the strings.

"*Can* you play?" asked Bob, grown suddenly suspicious, now that the man dare not prove his story.

"Can I *blay?*" he answered, with a quick lifting of his eyes, and the semblance of a smile lighting up his furrowed face. "I blay mit Strakosch te Mendelssohn Concerto in te olt Academy in Vourteenth Street; ant ven Alboni sing, no von in te virst violins haf te solo but me, ant dere is not a pin drop in te house, ant Madame Alboni send me all te flowers tey gif her. Can I BLAY!"

The tone of voice was masterly. He was a new experience to me, evidently an expert in this sort of thing. Bob looked down into his stagnant, inert face, noting the slightly scornful, hurt expression that lingered about the mouth. Then his tender heart got the better of him.

"I cannot afford to pay sixty dollars for another violin," he said, his voice expressing the sincerity of his regret.

"I cannot sell him vor less," replied the man, in a quick, decided way. It would have been an unfledged amateur impostor who could not have gained courage at this last change in Bob's tone. "Ven I get to New York," he continued, with almost a sob, "I must haf some money more as my railroad ticket to get anudder sheap violin. Te peoples will say it is Grossman come home vidout hees violin — he is broke. No, I no can sell him vor less. Tis cost one hundret ant sefenty-vive dollar ven I buy him."

I was about to offer him five dollars, buy the patched swindle, and end the affair — I had pressing business with Bob that morning — when he stopped me.

"Would you take thirty dollars and my old violin?"

The man looked at him eagerly.

"Vere is your violin?"

"At my house."

"Is it a goot von? Stop a minute" — For the third time he removed the old red silk handkerchief. "Draw te bow across vonce. I know aboud your violin ven I hears you blay."

Bob tucked the instrument under his chin and drew a full, clear, resonant tone.

The watery eyes glistened.

"Yes, I take your violin ant te money," in a decided tone. "You know 'em, ant I tink you loafe 'em too."

The subtle flattery of this last touch was exquisitely done. The man was an artist.

Bob reached for a pad, and, with the remark that he was wanted in court or he would go to his house with him, wrote an order, sealed it, and laid three ten-dollar bills on the table.

I felt that nothing now could check Bob. Whatever I might say or do would fail to convince him. "I know how hard a road can be and how sore one's feet can get," he would perhaps say to me, as he had often done before when we blamed him for his generosities.

The man balanced the letter on his hand, reading the inscription in a listless sort of way, picked up the instrument, looked it all over carefully, flecked off some specks of dust from the finger-board, laid the violin on the office table, thrust the soiled rag into his pocket, caught up the money, and without a word of thanks closed the door behind him.

"Bob," I said, the man's absolute ingratitude and my friend's colossal simplicity irritating me beyond control, "why in the name of common sense did you throw your money away on a sharp like that? Did n't you see through the whole game? That note was written by himself. Corunden never saw that fiddle in his life. You can buy a dozen of them for five dollars apiece in any pawnshop in town."

Bob looked at me with that peculiar softening of the eyelids which we know so well. Then he said thoughtfully: "Do you know what it is to be stranded in a strange city with not a cent in your pocket, afraid to look a policeman in the face lest he run you in? hungry, unwashed, not a clean shirt for weeks? I don't care if he is a fraud. He sha'n't go hungry if I can help it."

There are some episodes in Bob's life to which he seldom refers.

"Then why did n't he play for you?" I asked, still indignant, yet somewhat touched by an intense earnestness unusual in Bob.

"Yes, I wondered at that," he replied in a musing tone, but without a shadow of suspicion in his voice.

"You don't think," I continued, "he's such a fool as to go to your house for your violin? I'll bet you he's made a bee line for a rum mill; then he'll doctor up another old scraper and try the same game somewhere else. Let me go after him and bring him back."

Bob did not answer. He was tying up a bundle of papers. The violin lay on the green-baize table where the man had put it, the law books pushed aside to give it room. Then he put on his coat and went over to court.

In an hour he was back again — he and I, sitting in the small inner office overlooking the dingy courtyard.

We had talked but a few moments when a familiar shuffling step was heard in the corridor. I looked through the crack in the door, touched Bob's arm, and put my finger to my lips. Bob leaned forward and watched with me through the crack.

The outer office door was being slowly opened in the same noiseless way, and the same man was creeping in. He gave an anxious glance about the room. He had Bob's own violin in his hand; I knew it by the case.

"Tey all oud," he muttered in an undertone.

For an instant he wavered, looked hungrily towards his old violin, laid Bob's on a chair near the door, stepped on tiptoe to the green-baize table, picked up the Cremona, looked it all over, smoothing the back with his hands, then, nestling it under his chin, drew the bow gently across the strings, shut his eyes, and began the Concerto, — the one he had played with Alboni, — not with its full volume of sound or emphasis, but with echoes, pulsations, tremulous murmurings, faint breathings of its marvelous beauty. The instrument seemed part of himself, the neck welded to his fingers, the bow but a piece of his arm, with a heart-throb down its whole length.

When it was ended he rubbed his cheek softly against his old comrade, smoothed it once or twice with his hand, laid it tenderly back in its place on the table among the books, picked up Bob's violin from the chair, and gently closed the door behind him.

I looked at Bob. He was leaning against his desk, his eyes on the floor, his whole soul filled with the pathos of the melody. Suddenly he roused himself, sprang past me into the other room, and, calling to the man, ran out into the corridor.

"I could n't catch him," he said in a

dejected tone, coming back all out of breath, and dropping into a chair.

"What did you want to catch him for?" I asked; "he never robbed you?"

"Robbed me!" cried Bob, the tears starting to his eyes. "Robbed *me!* Good God, man! Could n't you hear? I robbed *him!*"

We searched for him all that day — Bob with the violin under his arm, I with an apology.

But he was gone.

ACCORDING TO THE LAW

I

THE luncheon was at one o'clock. Not one of your club luncheons, served in a silent, sedate mausoleum on the principal street, where your host in the hall below enters your name in a ledger, and a brass-be-buttoned Yellowplush precedes you upstairs into a desolate room furnished with chairs and a round table decorated with pink *boutonnières* set for six, and where you are plied with Manhattans until the other guests arrive.

Nor yet was it one of your smart petticoat luncheons in a Fifth Avenue mansion, where a Delmonico veteran pressed into service for the occasion waves you upstairs to another recruit, who deposits your coat and hat on a bed, and who later on ushers you into a room ablaze with gaslights — midday, remember — where you and the other unfortunates are served with English pheasants cooked in their own feathers, or Kennebec salmon embroidered with beets and appliqued with green mayonnaise. Not that kind of a midday meal at all.

On the contrary, it was served, — no, it was

eaten, — reveled in, made merry over, in an ancient house fronting on a sleepy old park filled with live oaks and magnolias, their trunks streaked with green moss and their branches draped with gray crape: an ancient house with a big white door that stood wide open to welcome you, — it was December, too, — and two verandas on either side, stretched out like welcoming arms, their railings half hidden in clinging roses, the blossoms in your face.

There was an old grandmother, too, — quaint as a miniature, — with fluffy white cap and a white worsted shawl and tea-rose cheeks, and a smile like an opening window, so sunny did it make her face. And how delightfully she welcomed us.

I can hear even now the very tones of her voice, and feel the soft, cool, restful touch of her hand.

And there was an old darky, black as a gum shoe, with tufts of grizzled gray wool glued to his temples — one of those loyal old house servants of the South who belong to a régime that is past. I watched him from the parlor scuffling with his feet as he limped along the wide hall to announce each new arrival (his master's old Madeira had foundered him, they said, years before), and always reaching the drawing-room door long after the newcomer had been welcomed by shouts of laughter and the open arms of every one in the room: the newcomer another girl, of course.

And this drawing-room, now I think of it, was not like any other drawing-room that I knew. Very few things in it matched. The carpet was a faded red, and of different shades of repair. The hangings were of yellow silk. There were haircloth sofas, and a big fireplace, and plenty of rocking chairs, and lounges covered with chintz of every pattern, and softened with cushions of every hue.

At one end hung a large mirror made of squares of glass laid like tiles in a dull gilt frame that had held it together for nearly a century, and on the same wall, too, and all so splotched and mouldy with age that the girls had to stoop down to pick out a pane clear enough to straighten their bonnets by.

And on the side wall there were family portraits, and over the mantel queer Chinese porcelains and a dingy coat-of-arms in a dingier frame, and on every table, in all kinds of dishes, flat and square and round, there were heaps and heaps of roses —

De Vonienses, Hermosas, and Agripinas — whose distinguished ancestors, hardy sons of the soil, came direct from the Mayflower (This shall not happen again), and who consequently never knew the enervating influences of a hothouse. And there were marble busts on pedestals, and a wonderful clock on high legs, and medallions with weeping willows of somebody's hair, besides a miscellaneous collection of large and small bric-à-brac, the heirlooms of five generations.

And yet, with all this mismatching of color, form, and style, — this chronological array of fittings and furnishings, beginning with the mouldy mirror and ending with the modern straw chair, — there was a harmony that satisfied one's every sense.

And so restful, and helpful, and comforting, and companionable was it all, and so accustomed was everything to be walked over, and sat on, and kicked about; so glad to be punched out of shape if it were a cushion which you needed for some special curve in your back or twist of your head; so delighted to be scratched, or slopped over, or scarred full of holes if it were a table that could hold your books or paste-pot or lighted pipe; so hilariously joyful to be stretched out of shape or sagged into irredeemable bulges if it were a straw chair that could sooth your aching bones or rest a tired muscle!

When all the girls and young fellows had arrived, — such pretty girls, with such soft, liquid voices and captivating dialects, the one their black mammies had taught them, — and such unconventional, happy young fellows in all sorts of costumes from blue flannel to broadcloth, — one in a Prince Albert coat and a straw hat in his hand, and it near Christmas, — the old darky grew more and more restless, limping in and out of the open door, dodging anxiously into the drawing-room and out again, his head up like a terrapin's.

Finally he veered across to a seat by the window, and, shielding his mouth with his wrinkled, leathery paw, bent over the old grandmother and poured into her ear a communication of such vital import that the dear old lady arose at once and, taking my hand, said in her low, sweet voice that we would wait no longer for the Judge, who was detained in court.

After this the aged Terrapin scuffled out again, reappearing almost immediately before the door in white gloves inches too long at the fingers. Then bowing himself backwards he preceded us into the dining-room.

And the table was so inviting when we took our seats around it, I sitting on the right of the grandmother — being the only stranger — and the prettiest of all the girls next to me. And the merriment was so contagious, and the sallies of wit so sparkling, and the table itself! Solid mahogany, this old heirloom! rich and dark as a meerschaum, the kind of mahogany that looked as if all the fine old Madeira and choice port that had been drunk above it had soaked into its pores. And every fibre of it in evidence, too, except where the silver coasters, and the huge silver centrepiece filled with roses, and the plates and the necessary appointments hid its shining countenance.

And the aged Terrapin evidently appreciated in full the sanctity of this family altar, and duly realized the importance of his position as its High Priest. Indeed, there was a gravity, a dignity, and repose about him as he limped through his ministrations which I had noticed in him before. If he showed any nervousness at all it was as he glanced now and then toward the drawing-room door through which the Judge must enter.

And yet he appeared outwardly calm, even under this strain. For had he not provided for every emergency? Were not His Honor's viands already at that moment on the kitchen hearth, with special plates over them to keep them hot against his arrival?

And what a luncheon it was! The relays of fried chicken, baked sweet potatoes, cornbread, and mango pickles — a most extraordinary production, I maintain, is a mango pickle! — and things baked on top and brown, and other things baked on the bottom and creamy white.

And the fun, too, as each course appeared and disappeared only to be followed by something more extraordinary and seductive. The men continued to talk, and the girls never ceased laughing, and the grandmother's eyes constantly followed the Terrapin, giving him mysterious orders with the slightest raising of an eyelash, and we had already reached the salad — or was it the baked ham? — when the fairy in the pink waist next me clapped her hands and cried out: —

"Oh, you dear Judge! We waited an hour for you" — it doubtless seemed long to her. "What in the world kept you?"

"Could n't help it, little one," came a voice in reply; and a man with silver-white hair, dignified bearing, and a sunny smile on his face edged his way around the table to the grandmother, every hand held out to him as he passed, and, bending low over the dear lady, expressed his regrets at having been detained.

Then with an extended hand to me and, "It gives me very great pleasure to see you in this part of the South, sir," he sat down in the vacant chair, nodding to everybody graciously as he spread his napkin. A moment later he leaned forward and said in explanation to the grandmother, —

"I waited for the jury to come in. You received my message, of course?"

"Oh, yes, dear Judge; and although we missed you we sat down at once."

"Have you been in court all day?" I asked as an introductory remark. Of course he had if he had waited for the jury. What an extraordinary collection of idiocies one could make if he jotted down all the stupid things said and heard when conversations were being opened.

"Yes, I am sorry to say, trying one of those cases which are becoming daily more common."

I looked up inquiringly.

"Oh, a negro, of course," and the Judge picked up his fork and moved back the wine glass.

"And such dreadful things happen, and such dreadful creatures are going about," said the grandmother, raising her hand deprecatingly.

"How do you account for it, madam?" I asked. "It was quite different before the war. I have often heard my father tell of the old days, and how much the masters did for their slaves, and how loyal their servants were. I remember one old servant whom we boys called Daddy Billy, who was really one of the family — quite like your" — and I nodded toward the Terrapin, who at the moment was pouring a thin stream of brown sherry into an equally attenuated glass for the special comfort and sustenance of the last arrival.

"Oh, you mean Mordecai," she interrupted, looking at the Terrapin. "He has always been one of our family. How long do you think he has lived with us?" — and she lowered her voice. "Forty-eight years — long before the war — and we love him dearly. My father gave him to us. No, it is not the old house servants, — it is these new negroes, born since the war, that make all the trouble."

"You are right, madam. They are not like Mordecai," and the Judge held up the thin glass between his eye and the light. "God bless the day when Mordecai was born! I think this is the Amazon sherry, is it not, my dear madam?"

"Yes, Mordecai's sherry, as we sometimes call it. It may interest you, sir, to hear about it," and she turned to me again. "This wine that the Judge praises so highly was once the pride of my husband's heart, and when Sherman came through and burned our homes, among the few things that were saved were sixty-two bottles of this old Amazon sherry, named after the ship that brought it over. Mordecai buried them in the woods and never told a single soul for two years after — not even my husband. There are a few bottles left, and I always bring one out when we have distinguished guests," and she bowed her head to the Judge and to me. "Oh, yes, Mordecai has always been one of our family, and so has his wife, who is almost as old as he is. She is in the kitchen now, and cooked this luncheon. If these new negroes would only behave like the old ones we would have no trouble," and a faint sigh escaped her.

The Terrapin, who during the conversation had disappeared in search of another hot course for the Judge, had now reappeared, and so the conversation was carried on in tones too low for his ears.

"And has any effort been made to bring these modern negroes, as you call them, into closer relation with you all, and"—

"It would be useless," interrupted the Judge. "The old negroes were held in check by their cabin life and the influence of the 'great house,' as the planter's home was called. All this has passed away. This new product has no home and wants none. They live like animals, and are ready for any crime. Sometimes I think they care neither for wife, child, nor any family tie. The situation is deplorable, and is getting worse every day. It is only the strong hand of the law that now controls these people." His Honor spoke with some positiveness, I thought, and with some warmth.

"But," I broke in, "if when things became more settled you had begun by treating them as your friends"—I was getting into shoal water, but I blundered on, peering into the fog — "and if you had not looked upon them as an alien race who" —

Just here the siren with the pink waist who sat next me — bless her sweet face! — blew her conch-shell — she had seen the rocks ahead — and cried out: —

"Now, grandma, please stop talking about the war!" (The dear lady had been silent for five minutes.) "We're tired and sick of it, are n't we, girls? And don't you say another word, Judge. You've got to tell us some stories."

A rattle of glasses from all the young people was the response, and the Judge rose, with his hand on his heart and his eyes upraised like those of a dying saint. He protested gallantly that he had n't said a word, and the grandmother insisted with a laugh that she had merely told me about Mordecai hiding the sherry, while I vowed with much solemnity that I had not once opened my lips since I sat down, and called upon the siren in pink to confirm it. To my great surprise she promptly did, with an arch look of mock reproof in her eye; whereupon, with an atoning bow to her, I grasped the lever, rang "full speed," and thus steamed out into deep water again.

While all this was going on at our end of

the table, a running fire of fun had been kept at the other end, near the young man in the Prince Albert coat, which soon developed into heavy practice, the Judge with infinite zest joining in the merriment, exploding one story after another, each followed by peals of laughter and each better than the other, his Honor eating his luncheon all the while with great gusto as he handled the battery.

During all this the Terrapin neglected no detail of his duty, but served the fifth course to the ladies and the kept-hot courses to the Judge with equal dexterity, and both at the same time, and all without spilling a drop or clinking a plate.

When the ladies had withdrawn and we were seated on the veranda fronting the sleepy old park, each man with a rose in his buttonhole, the gift of the girl who had sat next him (the grandmother had pinned the rose she wore at her throat on the lapel of the Judge's coat), and when the Terrapin had produced a silver tray and was about to fill some little egg-shell cups from a George-the-Third coffee-pot, the Judge, who was lying back in a straw chair, a picture of perfect repose and of peaceful digestion, turned his head slightly toward me and said, —

"I am sorry, sir, but I shall be obliged to leave you in a few minutes. I have to sentence a negro by the name of Sam Crouch. When these ladies can spare you it will give me very great pleasure to have you come into court and see how we administer justice to this much-abused and much-misunderstood race," and he smiled significantly at me.

"What was his crime, Judge?" asked the young man in the Prince Albert coat, as he held out his cup for Mordecai to fill. "Stealing chickens?" The gayety of the table was evidently still with him and upon him.

"No," replied the Judge gravely, and he looked at me, the faintest gleam of triumph in his eyes. "Murder."

II

THERE are contrasts in life, sudden transitions from light to dark, startling as those one experiences in dropping from out the light of a spring morning redolent with perfume into the gloom of a coal mine choked with noxious vapors — out of a morning, if you will, all joy and gladness and the music of many birds; a morning when the wide, white sky is filled with cloud ships drifting lazily; when the trees wave in the freshening wind, and the lark hanging in mid-air pours out its soul for very joy of living!

And the horror of that other! The never-ending night and silence; the foul air reeking with close, stifling odors; the narrow walls where men move as ghosts with heads alight, their bodies lost in the shadows; the ominous sounds of falling rock thundering through the blackness; and again, when all is still, the slow drop, drop of the ooze, like the tick of a deathwatch. It is a prison and a tomb, and to those who breathe the sweet air of heaven, and who love the sunshine, the very house of despair.

I myself experienced one of these contrasts when I exchanged all the love and gladness, all the wit and laughter and charm of the breakfast, for the court-room.

It was on the ground floor, level with the grass of the courtyard, which a sudden storm had just drenched. The approach was through a cold, crypt-like passage running under heavy brick arches. At its end hung a door blocked up with slouching ragged figures, craning their woolly heads for a glimpse inside whenever some official or visitor passed in or out.

I elbowed my way past the constables holding long staffs, and, standing on my toes, looked over a sea of heads — a compact mass wedged together as far down as the rail outside the bench. The air was sickening, loathsome, almost unbreathable. The only light, except the dull gray light of the day, came from a single gas jet flaring over the Judge's head. Every other part of the courtroom was lost in the shadow of the passing storm.

Inside the space where the lawyers sat, the floor was littered with torn papers, and the tables were heaped with bundles of briefs and law books in disorder, many of them opened face down.

Behind me rose the gallery reserved for negroes, a loft having no window nor light, hanging like a huge black shadow without form or outline. All over this huge black shadow were spattered specks of white. As I looked again, I could see that these were the strained eyeballs and set teeth of motionless negroes.

The Judge, his hands loosely clasped together, sat leaning forward in his seat, his eyes fastened on the prisoner. The flare of the gas jet fell on his stern, immobile face, and cast clear-lined shadows that cut his profile sharp as a cameo.

The negro stood below him, his head on

his chest, his arms hanging straight. On either side, close within reach of the doomed man, were the sheriffs — rough-looking men, with silver shields on their breasts. They looked straight at the Judge, nodding mechanically as each word fell from his lips. They knew the litany.

The condemned man was evidently under thirty years of age, of almost pure African blood, well built, and strong. The forehead was low, the lips heavy, the jaw firm. The brown-black face showed no cruelty; the eyes were not cunning. It was only a dull, inert face, like those of a dozen others about him.

As he turned again, I saw that his hair was cut short, revealing lighter-colored scars on the scalp — records of a not too peaceful life, perhaps. His dress was ragged and dingy, patched trousers, and shabby shoes, and a worn flannel shirt open at the throat, the skin darker than the flannel. On a chair beside him lay a crumpled slouch hat, grimed with dirt, the crown frayed and torn.

As I pressed my way farther into the throng toward the bench, the voice of the Judge rose, filling every part of the room, the words falling slowly, as earth drops upon a coffin: —

—"until you be dead, and may God have mercy on your soul!"

I looked searchingly into the speaker's face. There was not an expression that I could recall, nor a tone in his voice that I remembered. Surely this could not be the same man I had met at the table but an hour before, with that musical laugh and winning smile. I scrutinized him more closely—the rose was still in his buttonhole.

As the voice ceased, the condemned man lifted his face, and turned his head slowly. For a moment his eyes rested on the Judge; then they moved to the clerks, sitting silent and motionless; then behind, at the constables, and then up into the black vault packed with his own people.

A deathlike silence met him everywhere.

One of the officers stepped closer. The condemned man riveted his gaze upon him, and held out his hands helplessly; the officer leaned forward, and adjusted the handcuffs. Then came the sharp click of their teeth, like the snap of a hungry wolf.

The two men,—the criminal judged according to the law, and the sheriff, its executor,—chained by their wrists, wheeled about and faced the crowd. The constables raised their staffs, formed a guard, and forced a way through the crowd, the silent gallery following with their eyes until the door closed upon them.

Then through the gloom there ran the audible shiver of pent-up sighs, low whispers, and the stretching of tired muscles.

When I reached the Judge, he was just entering the door of the anteroom opening into his private quarters. His sunny smile had returned, although the voice had not altogether regained its former ring. He said, —

"I trust you were not too late. I waited a few minutes, hoping you had come, and then when it became so dark, I ordered a light lit, but I could n't find you in the crowd. Come in. Let me present you to the district attorney and to the young lawyer whom I appointed to defend the prisoner. While I was passing sentence, they were discussing the verdict. Were you in time for the sentence?" he continued.

"No," I answered, after shaking hands with both gentlemen and taking the chair which one of them offered me, "only the last part. But I saw the man before they led him away, and I must say he did n't look much like a criminal. Tell me something about the murder," and I turned to the young lawyer, a smooth-faced young man with long black hair tucked behind his ears and a frank, open countenance.

"You 'd better ask the district attorney," he answered, with a slight shrug of his shoulders. "He is the only one about here who seems to know anything about the *murder;* my client, Crouch, did n't, anyhow. I was counsel for the defense."

He spoke with some feeling, and I thought with some irritation, but whether because of his chagrin at losing the case or because of real sympathy for the negro I could not tell.

"You seem to forget the jury," answered the district attorney in a self-satisfied way; "they evidently knew something about it." There was a certain elation in his manner, as he spoke, that surprised me—quite as if he had won a bet. That a life had been played for and lost seemed only to heighten his interest in the game.

"No, I don't forget the jury," retorted the young man, "and I don't forget some of the witnesses; nor do I forget what you made them say and how you got some of them tangled up. That negro is as innocent of that crime as I am. Don't you think so, Judge?" and he turned to the table and began gathering up his papers.

His Honor had settled himself in his chair,

the back tipped against the wall. His old manner had returned, so had the charm of his voice. He had picked up a reed pipe when he entered the room, and had filled it with tobacco, which he had broken in finer grains in the palm of his hand. He was now puffing away steadily to keep it alight.

"I have no opinion to offer, gentlemen, one way or the other. The matter, of course, is closed as far as I am concerned. I think you will both agree, however, whatever may be your personal feelings, that my rulings were fair. As far as I could see, the witnesses told a straight story, and upon their evidence the jury brought in the verdict. I think, too, my charge was just. There was" — here the Judge puffed away vigorously — "there was, therefore, nothing left for me to do but" — puff — puff — "to sentence him. Hang that pipe! It won't draw," and the Judge, with one of his musical laughs, rose from his chair and pulled a straw from the broom in the corner.

The district attorney looked at the discomfited opposing counsel and laughed. Then he added, as an expression of ill-concealed contempt for his inexperience crept over his face: —

"Don't worry over it, my boy. This is one of your first cases, and I know it comes hard, but you 'll get over it before you 've tried as many of them as I have. The nigger had n't a dollar, and somebody had to defend him. The Judge appointed you, and you 've done your duty well, and lost — that 's all there is to it. But I 'll tell you one thing for your information," — and his voice assumed a serious tone, — "and one which you did not notice in this trial, and which you would have done had you known the ways of these niggers as I do, and it went a long way with me in establishing his guilt. From the time Crouch was arrested, down to this very afternoon when the Judge sentenced him, not one of his people has ever turned up, — no father, mother, wife, nor child, — not one."

"That 's not news to me," interrupted the young man. "I tried to get something from Crouch myself, but he would n't talk."

"Of course he would n't talk, and you know why; simply because he did n't want to be spotted for some other crime. This nigger Crouch" — and the district attorney looked my way — "is a product of the war, and one of the worst it has given us — a shiftless tramp that preys on society." His remarks were evidently intended for me, for the Judge was not listening, nor was the young lawyer. "Most of this class of criminals have no homes, and if they had they lie about them, so afraid are they, if they 're fortunate enough to be discharged, that they 'll be rearrested for a crime committed somewhere else."

"Which discharge does n't very often happen around here," remarked the young man with a sneer. "Not if you can help it."

"No, which does n't very often happen around here *if I can help it.* You 're right. That 's what I 'm here for," the district attorney retorted with some irritation. "And now I 'll tell you another thing. I had a second talk with Crouch only this afternoon after the verdict" — and he turned to me — "while the Judge was lunching with you, sir, and I begged him, now that it was all over, to send for his people, but he was stubborn as a mule, and swore he had no one who would want to see him. I don't suppose he had; he 's been an outcast since he was born."

"And that 's why you worked so hard to hang him, was it?" The young man was thoroughly angry. I could see the color mount to his cheeks. I could see, too, that Crouch had no friends, except this young sprig of the law, who seemed as much chagrined over the loss of his case as anything else. And yet, I confess, I did not let my sympathies for the under dog get the better of me. I knew enough of the record of this new race not to recognize that there could be two sides to questions like this.

The district attorney bit his lip at the young man's thrust. Then he answered him slowly, but without any show of anger: —

"You have one thing left, you know. You can ask for a new trial. What do you say, Judge?"

The Judge made no answer. He evidently had lost all interest in the case, for during the discussion he had been engaged in twisting the end of the straw into the stem of the pipe and peering into the clogged bowl with one eye shut.

"And if the Judge granted it, what good would it do?" burst out the young man as he rose to his feet. "If Sam Crouch had a soul as white as snow, it would n't help him with these juries around here as long as his skin is the color it is!" and he put on his hat and left the room.

The Judge looked after him a moment and then said to me, —

"Our young men, sir, are impetuous and outspoken, but their hearts are all right. I have n't a doubt but that Crouch was guilty. He 's probably been a vagrant all his life."

III

SOME weeks after these occurrences I was on my way South, and again found myself within reach of the sleepy old park and the gruesome court-room.

I was the only passenger in the Pullman. I had traveled all night in this royal fashion — a whole car to myself — with the porter, a quiet, attentive young colored man of perhaps thirty years of age, duly installed as First Gentleman of the Bedchamber, and I had settled myself for a morning of seclusion when my privacy was broken in upon at a way station by the entrance of a young man in a shooting jacket and cap, and high boots splashed with mud.

He carried a folding gun in a leather case, an overcoat, and a game-bag, and was followed by two dogs. The porter relieved him of his belongings, stowed his gun in the rack, hung his overcoat on the hook, and distributed the rest of his equipment within reach of his hand. Then he led the dogs back to the baggage car.

The next moment the young sportsman glanced over the car, rose from his seat, and held out his hand.

"Have n't forgotten me, have you? Met you at the luncheon, you know — time the Judge was late waiting for the jury to come in."

To my delight and astonishment it was the young man in the Prince Albert coat.

He proved, as the morning wore on, to be a most entertaining young fellow, telling me of his sport and the birds he had shot, and of how good one dog was and how stupid the other, and how next week he was going after ducks down the river, and he described a small club-house which a dozen of his friends had built, and where, with true Southern hospitality, he insisted I should join him.

And then we fell to talking about the luncheon, and what a charming morning we had spent, and of the pretty girls and the dear grandmother; and we laughed again over the Judge's stories, and he told me another, the Judge's last, which he had heard his Honor tell at another luncheon;

and then the porter put up a table, and spread a cloth, and began opening things with a corkscrew, and filling empty glasses with crushed ice and other things, and altogether we had a most comfortable and fraternal and much-to-be-desired half hour.

Just before he left the train — he had to get out at the junction — some further reference to the Judge brought to my recollection that ghostly afternoon in the courtroom. Suddenly the picture of the negro with that look of stolid resignation on his face came before me. I asked him if any appeal had been taken in the case as suggested by the district attorney.

"Appeal? In the Crouch case? Not much. Hung him high as Haman."

"When?"

"'Bout a week ago. And by the way, a very curious thing happened at the hanging. The first time they strung Crouch up the rope broke and let him down, and they had to send eight miles for another. While they were waiting the mail arrived. The post-office was right opposite. In the bag was a letter for Crouch, care of the warden, but not directed to the jail. The postmaster brought it over and the warden opened it and read it to the prisoner, asking him who it was from, and the nigger said it was from his mother — that the man she worked for had written it. Of course the warden knew it was from Crouch's girl, for Crouch had always sworn he had no family, so the Judge told me. Then Crouch asked the warden if he 'd answer it for him before he died. The warden said he would, and got a sheet of paper, a pen and ink, and sitting down by Crouch under the gallows asked him what he wanted to say. And now, here comes the funny part. All that negro wanted to say was just this : —

" 'I 'm enjoying good health and I hope to see you before long.' SAM CROUCH.'

"Then Crouch reached over and took the pen out of the warden's hands, and marked a cross underneath what the warden had written, and when the warden asked him what he did that for, he said he wanted his mother to have something he had touched himself. By that time the new rope came and they swung him up. Curious, was n't it? The warden said it was the funniest message he ever knew a dying nigger to send, and he 'd hung a good many of 'em. It struck me as being some secret kind of a password. You never can tell about these coons."

"Did the warden mail it?"

"Oh, yes, of course he mailed it — warden 's square as a brick. Sent it, of course, care of the man the girl works for. He lives somewhere around here, or Crouch said he did. Awfully glad to see you again — I get out here."

The porter brought in the dogs, I picked up the gun, and we conducted the young sportsman out of the car and into a buggy waiting for him at the end of the platform.

As I entered the car again and waved my hand to him from the open window, I saw a negro woman dart from out the crowd of loungers, as if in eager search of some one. She was a tall, bony, ill-formed woman, wearing the rude garb of a farm hand — blue cotton gown, brown sunbonnet, and the rough muddy shoes of a man.

The dress was faded almost white in parts, and patched with different colors, but looked fresh and clean. It was held together over her flat bust by big bone buttons. There was neither collar nor belt. The sleeves were rolled up above the elbows, showing her strong, muscular arms, tough as rawhide. The hands were large and bony, with big knuckles, the mark of the hoe in the palms.

In her eagerness to speak to the porter the sunbonnet had slipped off. Black as the face was, it brought to my mind, strange to say, those weather-tanned fishwives of the Normandy coast — those sturdy, patient, earnest women, accustomed to toil and exposure and to the buffetings of wind and tempest.

When the porter appeared on his way back to the car, she sprang forward, and caught him by the arm.

"Oh, I'm dat sorry! An' he ain't come wid ye?" she cried. "But ye see him, did n't ye?" The voice was singularly sweet and musical. "Ye did? Oh, dat's good."

As she spoke, a little black bare-legged pickaninny, with one garment, ran out from behind the corner of the station, and clung to the woman's skirts, hiding her face in their folds. The woman put her hard, black hand on the child's cheek, and drew the little woolly head closer to her side.

"Well, when's he comin'? I come dis mawnin' jes 's ye tol' me. An' ye see him, did ye?" she asked with a strange quivering pathos in her voice.

"Oh, yes, I see him yisterday."

The porter's answer was barely audible. I

noticed, too, that he looked away from her as he spoke.

"An' yer sho' now he ain't come wid ye," and she looked toward the train as if expecting to find some one.

"No, he can't come till nex' Saturday," answered the porter.

"Well, I 'm mighty dis'pinted. I been a-waitin' an' a-waitin' till I *mos'* gin out. Ain't nobody helped me like him. You tol' me las' time dat he 'd be here to-day," and her voice shook. "You tell him I got his letter an' dat I think 'bout him night an' day, an' dat I 'd rudder see him dan anybody in de worl'. And you tell him — an' doan' ye forgit dis — dat you see his sister Maria's chile — dis is her — hol' up yer haid, honey, an' let him see ye. I thought if he come to-day he 'd like to see 'er, 'cause he useter tote her roun' on his back when she war n't big'r 'n a shote. An' ye *see* him, did ye? Well, I 'm mighty glad o' dat."

She was bending forward, her great black hand on his wrist, her eyes fixed on his. Then a startled, anxious look crossed her face.

"But he ain't sick dat he did n't come? Yo' *sho'* now, he ain't sick?"

"Oh, no; never see him lookin' so good."

The porter was evidently anxious about the train, for he kept backing away toward his car.

"Well, den, good-by; but doan' ye forgit. Tell him ye see me an' dat I 'm a-hungerin' for him. You hear, *a-hungerin'* for him, an' dat I can't git 'long no mo' widout him. Don' ye forgit, now, 'cause I mos' daid a-waitin' for him. Good-by."

The train rolled on. She was still on the platform, her gaunt figure outlined against the morning sky, her eager eyes strained toward us, the child clutching her skirts.

. . . .

I confess that I have never yet outgrown my affection for the colored race: an affection at best, perhaps, born of the dim, undefined memories of my childhood and of an old black mammy — my father's slave — who crooned over me all day long, and sang me lullabies at night.

I am aware, too, that I do not always carry this affectionate sympathy locked up in a safe, but generally pinned on the outside of my sleeve; and so it is not surprising, as the hours wore on, and the porter gradually developed his several capacities for making me comfortable, that a certain confidence was established between us.

According to the Law

Then, again, I have always looked upon a Pullman porter as a superior kind of person — certainly among serving people. He does not often think so himself, nor does he ever present to the average mind any marked signs of genius. He is in appearance and deportment very much like all other uniformed attendants belonging to most of the great corporations; clean, neatly dressed, polite, watchful, and patient. He is also indiscriminate in his ministrations; for he will gladly open the window for No. 10, and as cheerfully close it one minute later for No. 6. After traveling with him for half a day, you doubtless conclude that nothing more serious weighs on his mind than the duty of regulating the temperature of his car, or looking after its linen. But you are wrong.

All this time he is classifying you. He really located you when you entered the car, summing you up as you sought out your berth number. At his first glance he had divined your station in life by your clothes, your personal refinement, by your carpet-bag, and your familiarity with travel by the way you took your seat. The shoes he will black for you in the still small hours of the morning, when he has time to think, will give him any other points he requires.

According to the Law

If they are patched or half-soled, no amount of diamond shirt studs or watch chain worn with them will save your respectability. If you should reverse your cuffs before him, or imbibe your stimulants from a black bottle which you carry in your inside pocket instead of a silver flask concealed in your bag, no amount of fees will gain for you his unqualified respect. If none of these delinquencies can be laid to your account, and he is still in doubt, he waits until you open your bag.

Should the first rapid glance betray your cigars packed next to your shoes, or the handle of a toothbrush thrust into the sponge-bag, or some other such violation of his standard, your status is fixed; he knows you. And he does all this while he is bowing and smiling, bringing you a pillow for your head, opening a transom, or putting up wire screens to save you from draughts and dust, and all without any apparent distinction between you and your fellow passengers.

If you swear at him, he will not answer back, and if you smite him, he will nine times out of ten turn to you the other cheek. He does all this because his skin is black, and yours is white, and because he is the servant and representative of a corporation who will see him righted, and who are accustomed to hear complaints. Above all, he will do so because of the wife and children or mother at home in need of the money he earns, and destined to suffer if he lose his place.

He has had, too, if you did but know it, a life as interesting, perhaps, as any of your acquaintances. It is quite within the possibilities that he has been once or twice to Spain, Italy, or Egypt, depending on the movements of the master he served; that he can speak a dozen words or more of Spanish or Italian or pigeon English, and oftener than not the best English of our public schools; can make an omelette, sew on a button, or clean a gun, and that in an emergency or accident (I know of two who lost their lives to save their passengers) he can be the most helpful, the most loyal, the most human serving man and friend you can find the world over.

If you are selfishly intent on your own affairs, and look upon his civility and his desire to please you as included in the price of your berth or seat, and decide that any extra service he may render you is canceled by the miserable twenty-five cents which you give him, you will know none of these accomplishments nor the spirit that rules them.

If, however, you are the kind of man who

goes about the world with your heart unbuttoned and your earflaps open, eager to catch and hold any little touch of pathos or flash of humor or note of tragedy, you cannot do better than gain his confidence.

. . . .

I cannot say by what process I accomplished this result with this particular porter and on this particular train. It may have been the newness of my shoes, combined with the proper stowing of my toothbrush and the faultless cut of my pajamas; or it might have been the fact that he had already divined that I liked his race; but certain it is that no sooner was the woman out of sight than he came direct to my seat, and, with a quiver in his voice, said, —

"Did you see dat woman I spoke to, suh?"

"Yes; you did n't seem to want to talk to her."

"Oh, it war n't dat, suh, but dat woman 'bout breaks my heart. Had n't been for de gemman gettin' off here an' me havin' to get his dogs, I would n't 'a' got out de car at all. I hoped she would n't come to-day. I thought she heared 'bout it. Everybody knows it up an' down de road, an' de papers been full, tho' co'se she can't read. She lives 'bout ten miles from here, an' she walked in dis mawnin'. Comes every Saturday. I only makes dis run on Saturday, and she knows de day I 'm comin'."

"Some trouble?" I asked.

"Oh, yes, suh, a heap o' trouble; mo' trouble dan she kin stan' when she knows it. Beats all why nobody ain't done tol' her. I been talkin' to her every Saturday now for a month, tellin' her I see him an' dat he 's a-comin' down, an' dat he sent her his love, an' once or twice lately I 'd bring her li'l' things he sent her. Co'se *he* did n't send 'em, 'cause he was whar he could n't get to 'em, but she did n't know no better. He 's de only son now she 'd got, an' he 's been mighty good to her an' dat li'l' chile she had wid her. I knowed him ever since he worked on de railroad. Mos' all de money he gits he gives to her. If he done the thing they said he done I ain't got nothin' mo' to say, but I don't believe he done it, an' never will. I thought maybe dey 'd let him go, an' den he 'd come home, an' she would n't have to suffer no mo'; dat made me keep on a-lyin' to her."

"What 's been the matter? Has he been arrested?"

"'Rested! *'Rested!* Fo' God, suh, dey done hung him las' week."

A light began to break in upon me.

According to the Law

"What was his name?"

"Same name as his mother's, suh — Sam Crouch."

"NEVER HAD NO SLEEP"

IT was on the upper deck of a Chesapeake Bay boat, *en route* for Old Point Comfort and Norfolk. I was bound for Norfolk.

"Kinder ca'm, ain't it?"

The voice proceeded from a pinched-up old fellow with a colorless face, straggling white beard, and sharp eyes. He wore a flat-topped slouch hat resting on his ears, and a red silk handkerchief tied in a sporting knot around his neck. His teeth were missing, the lips puckered up like the mouth of a sponge-bag. In his hand he carried a cane with a round ivory handle. This served as a prop to his mouth, the puckered lips fumbling about the knob. He was shadowed by an old woman wearing a shiny brown silk, that glistened like a wet waterproof, black mitts, poke-bonnet, flat lace collar, and a long gold watch chain. I had noticed them at supper. She was cutting up his food.

"Kinder ca'm, ain't it?" he exclaimed again, looking my way. "Fust real nat'ral vittles I 've eat fur a year. Spect it 's ther sea air. This water 's brackish, ain't it?"

I confirmed his diagnosis of the saline

qualities of the Chesapeake, and asked if he had been an invalid. *"Never had no Sleep"*

"Waal, I should say so! Bin livin' on hospital mush fur nigh on ter a year; but, by gum! ter-night I jist said ter Mommie: 'Mommie, shuv them soft-shells this way. Ain't seen none sence I kep' tavern.'"

Mommie nodded her head in confirmation, but with an air of "if you're dead in the morning, don't blame me."

"What's been the trouble?" I inquired, drawing up a camp stool.

"Waal, I dunno rightly. Got my stummic out o' gear, throat kinder weak, and what with the seventies"—

"Seventies?" I asked.

"Yes; hed 'em four year. I'm seventy-five nex' buthday. But come ter sum it all up, what's ther matter with me is I ain't never had no sleep. Let me sit on t'other side. One ear's stopped workin' this ten year."

He moved across and pulled an old cloak around him.

"Been long without sleep?" I asked sympathetically.

"'Bout sixty year — mebbe sixty-five."

I looked at him inquiringly, fearing to break the thread if I jarred too heavily.

"Never had no Sleep"

"Yes, spect it must be more. Well, you keep tally. Five year bootblack and porter in a tavern in Dover, 'leven year tendin' bar down in Wilmington, fourteen year bootcherin', nineteen year an' six months keepin' a roadhouse ten miles from Philadelphy fur ther hucksters comin' to market — quit las' summer. How much yer got?"

I nodded, assenting to his estimate of sixty-five years of service, if he had started when fifteen.

He ruminated for a time, caressing the ivory ball of his cane with his uncertain mouth.

I jogged him again. "Boots and tending bar I should think would be wakeful, but I did n't suppose butchering and keeping hotel necessitated late hours."

"Well, that 's 'cause yer don't know. Bootcherin 's ther wakefulest business as is. Now yer a country bootcher, mind — no city beef man, nor porter-house steak and lamb chops fur clubs an' hotels, but jest an all-round bootcher — lamb, veal, beef, mebbe once a week, ha'f er whole, as yer trade goes. Now ye kill when ther sun goes down, so ther flies can't mummuck 'em. Next yer head and leg 'em, gittin' in in rough, as we call it — takin' out ther insides an' leavin' ther hide on ther back. Ye let 'em hang fur four hours, and 'bout midnight ye go at 'em agin, trim an' quarter, an' 'bout four in winter and three in summer ye open up ther stable with a lantern, git yer stuff in, an' begin yer rounds."

"Never had no Sleep"

"Yes, I see; but keeping hotel is n't"—

"Now thar ye 're dead out agin. Ye 're a-keepin' a roadhouse, mind—one of them huckster taverns where ha'f yer folks come in 'arly 'bout sundown and sit up ha'f ther night, and t'other ha'f drive inter yer yard 'bout midnight an' lie round till daybreak. It 's eat er drink all ther time, and by ther time ye 've stood behind ther bar and jerked down ev'ry bottle on ther shelf, gone out ha'f a dozen times with er light ter keep some mule from kickin' out yer partitions, got er dozen winks on er settee in a back room, and then begin bawlin' upstairs, routin' out two or three hired gals to get 'arly breakfust, ye 're nigh tuckered out. By ther time this gang is fed, here comes another drivin' in. Oh, thet 's a nice quiet life, thet is! I quit las' year, and me and Mommie is on our way to Old P'int Cumfut. I ain't never bin thar, but ther name sounded peaceful like, and so I tho't ter try it. I 'm in sarch er sleep, I am. Wust

"Never had no Sleep"

thing 'bout me is, no matter whar I 'm lyin', when it comes three 'clock I 'm out of bed. Bin at it all my life; can't never break it."

"But you 've enjoyed life?" I interpolated.

"Enj'yed life! Well, p'rhaps, and agin p'rhaps not," looking furtively at his wife. Then, lowering his voice: "There ain't bin er horse race within er hundred miles of Philadelphy I ain't tuk in. Enj'y! Well, don't yer worry." And his sharp eyes snapped.

I believed him. That accounted for the way the red handkerchief was tied loosely round his throat — an old road-wagon trick to keep the dust out.

For some minutes he nursed his knees with his hands, rocking himself to and fro, smiling gleefully, thinking, no doubt, of the days he had speeded down the turnpike, and the seats, too, on the grand stand.

I jogged him again, venturing the remark that I should think that now he might try and corral a nap in the daytime.

The gleeful expression faded instantly. "See here," he said seriously, laying his hand with a warning gesture on my arm, the ivory knob popping out of the sponge-bag. "Don't yer never take no sleep in ther daytime; that 's suicide. An' if yer sleep after eatin', that 's murder. Look at me. Kinder peaked, ain't I? Stummic gone, throat busted, mouth caved in; but I 'm seventy-five, ain't I? An' I ain't a wreck yet, am I? An' a-goin' to Old P'int Cumfut, ain't we, me an' Mommie, who 's sixty — Never mind, Mommie. I won't give it away" — with a sly wink at me. The old woman looked relieved. "Now jist s'pose I 'd sat all my life on my back stoop, ha'f awake, an' ev'ry time I eat, lie down an' go ter sleep. Waal, yer 'd never bin talkin' to-night to old Jeb Walters. They 'd 'a' bin fertilizin' gardin truck with him. I 've seen more 'n a dozen of my friends die thet way — busted on this back porch snoozin' business. Fust they git loggy 'bout ther gills; then their knees begin ter swell; purty soon they 're hobblin' round on er cane; an' fust thing they know they 're tucked away in er number thirteen coffin, an' ther daisies a-bloomin' over 'em. None er that fur me. Come, Mommie, we 'll turn in."

"Never had no Sleep"

When the boat, next morning, touched the pier at Old Point, I met the old fellow and his wife waiting for the plank to be hauled aboard.

"Never had no Sleep"

"Did you sleep?" I asked.

"Sleep? Waal, I could, p'rhaps, if I knowed ther ways aboard this steamboat. Ther come er nigger to my room 'bout midnight, and wanted ter know if I was ther gentleman that had lost his carpet-bag — he had it with him. Waal, of course I warn't; and then 'bout three, jist as I tho't I was dozin' off agin, ther come ther dangdest poundin' the nex' room ter mine ye ever heard. Mommie, she said 't was fire, but I did n't smell no smoke. Wrong room agin. Feller nex' door was to go ashore in a scow with some dogs and guns. They 'd a-slowed down and was waitin', an' they could n't wake him up. Mebbe I 'll git some sleep down ter Old P'int Cumfut, but I ain't spectin' nuthin'. By, by."

And he disappeared down the gang plank.

THE MAN WITH THE EMPTY SLEEVE

I

THE Doctor closed the book with an angry gesture and handed it to me as I lay in my steamer chair, my eyes on the tumbling sea. He had read every line in it. So had P. Wooverman Shaw Todd, Esquire, whose property it was, and who had announced himself only a moment before as heartily in sympathy with the pessimistic views of the author, especially in those chapters which described domestic life in America.

The Doctor, who has a wrist of steel and a set of fingers steady enough to adjust a chronometer, and who, though calm and silent as a stone god when over an operating table, is often as restless and outspoken as a boy when something away from it touches his heartstrings, turned to me and said: —

"There ought to be a law passed to keep these men out of the United States. Here's a Frenchman, now, who speaks no language but his own, and after spending a week at Newport, another at New York, two days at Niagara, and then rushing through the West on a 'Limited,' goes home to give his Impressions of America. Read that chapter on Manners," and he stretched a hand over my shoulder, turning the leaves quickly with his fingers. "You would think, to listen to these fellows, that all there is to a man is the cut of his coat or the way he takes his soup. Not a line about his being clean and square and alive and all a man, — just manners! Why, it is enough to make a cast-iron dog bite a blind man."

It would be a waste of time to criticise the Doctor for these irrelevant verbal explosives. Indefensible as they are, they are as much parts of his individuality as the deftness of his touch and the fearlessness of his methods are parts of his surgical training.

P. Wooverman Shaw Todd, Esquire, looked at the Doctor with a slight lifting of his upper lip and a commiserating droop of the eyelid, — an expression indicating, of course, a consciousness of that superior birth and breeding which prevented the possibility of such outbreaks. It was a manner he sometimes assumed toward the Doctor, although they were good friends. P. Wooverman and the Doctor are fellow townsmen and members of the same set, and members, too, of the same club, — a most exclusive club of one hundred. The Doctor had gained admission, not because of his ancestors, etc. (see Log of the Mayflower), but because he had been the first and only American surgeon who had removed some very desirable portions of a gentleman's interior, had washed and ironed them and scalloped their edges, for all I know, and had then replaced them, without being obliged to sign the patient's death certificate the next day.

P. Wooverman Shaw Todd, Esquire, on the other hand, had gained admission because of — well, Todd's birth and his position (he came of an old Salem family who did something in whale oil, — not fish or groceries, be it understood); his faultless attire, correct speech, and knowledge of manners and men; his ability to spend his summers in England and his winters in Nice; his extensive acquaintance among distinguished people, — the very most distinguished, I know, for Todd has told me so himself, — and — well, all these must certainly be considered sufficient qualifications to entitle any man to membership in almost any club in the world.

P. Wooverman Shaw Todd, Esquire, I say, elevated his upper lip and drooped his eyelid, remarking with a slight Beacon Street accent: —

"I cawn't agree with you, my dear Doctor," — there were often traces of the manners and the bearing of a member of the Upper House in Todd, especially when he talked to a man like the Doctor, who wore turned-down collars and detached cuffs, and who, to quote the distinguished Bostonian, "threw words about like a coal heaver," — "I cawn't agree with you, I say. It is n't the obzervar that we should criticise; it is what he finds." P. Wooverman was speaking with his best accent. Somehow, the Doctor's bluntness made him over-accentuate it, — particularly when there were listeners about. "This French critic is a man of distinction and a member of the most excloosive circles in Europe. I have met him myself repeatedly, although I cawn't say I know him. We Americans are too sensitive, my dear Doctor. His book, to me, is the work of a keen obzervar who knows the world, and who sees how woefully lacking we are in some of the common civilities of life," and he smiled faintly at me, as if confident that I shared his opinion of the Doctor's own shortcomings. "This Frenchman does not lay it on a bit too thick. Nothing is so mortifying to me as being obliged to travel with a party of Americans who are making their first tour abroad. And it is quite impossible to avoid them, for they all have money and can go where they please. I remember once coming from Basle to Paris, in a first-class carriage, — it was only larst summer, — with a fellow from Indiana or Michigan, or somewhere out there. He had a wife with him who looked like a cook, and a daughter about ten years old, who was a most objectionable young person. You could hear them talk all over the train. I should n't have minded it so much, but Lord Norton's harf-brother was with me," — and P. Wooverman Shaw Todd glanced, as he spoke, at a thin lady with a smelling bottle and an air of reserve, who always sat with a maid beside her, to see if she were looking at him, — "and one of the best bred men in England, too, and a man who" —

"Now hold on, Todd," broke in the Doctor, upon whom neither the thin lady nor any other listener had made the slightest impression. "No glittering generalities with me. Just tell me in so many plain words what this man's vulgarity consisted of."

"Why, his manners, his dress, Doctor, — everything about him," retorted Todd.

"Just as I thought! All you think about is manners, only manners!" exploded the

Doctor. "Your Westerner, no doubt, was a hard-fisted, weather-tanned farmer, who had worked all his life to get money enough to take his wife and child abroad. The wife had tended the dairy and no doubt milked ten cows, and in their old age they both wanted to see something of the world they had heard about. So off they go. If you had any common sense or anything that brought you in touch with your kind, Todd, and had met that man on his own level, instead of overawing him with your high-daddy airs, he would have told you that both the wife and he were determined that the little girl should have a better start in life than their own, and that this trip was part of her education. Do you know any other working people,"—and the Doctor faced him squarely,—"any Dutch, or French, or English, Esquimaux or Hottentots, who take their wives and children ten thousand miles to educate them? If I had my way with the shaping of the higher education of the country, the first thing I would teach a boy would be to learn to work, and with his hands, too. We have raised our heroes from the soil,—not from the easy-chairs of our clubs,"—and he looked at Todd with his eyebrows knotted tight. "Let the boy get down and smell the earth, and let him get down to the level of his kind, helping the weaker man all the time and never forgetting the other fellow. When he learns to do this he will begin to know what it is to be a man, and not a manikin."

When the Doctor is mounted on any one of his hobbies, — whether it is a new microbe, Wagner, or the rights of the workingman, — he is apt to take the bit in his teeth and clear fences. As he finished speaking, two or three of the occupants of contiguous chairs laid down their books to listen. The thin lady with the smelling bottle and the maid remarked in an undertone to another exclusive passenger on the other side of her, in diamonds and white ermine cape, — it was raining at the time, — that "one need not travel in a first-class carriage to find vulgar Americans," and she glanced from the Doctor to a group of young girls and young men who were laughing as heartily and as merrily, and perhaps as noisily, as if they were sitting on their own front porches at their Southern homes.

Another passenger — who turned out later to be a college professor — said casually, this time to me, that he thought good and bad manners were to be determined, not by externals, but by what lay underneath; that neither dress, language, nor habits fixed or marred the standard. "A high-class Turk, now," and he lowered his voice, "would be considered ill bred by some people, because in the seclusion of his own family he helps himself with his fingers from the common dish; and yet so punctiliously polite and courteous is he that he never sits down in his father's presence nor lights a cigarette without craving his permission."

After this the talk became general, the group taking sides; some supporting the outspoken Doctor in his blunt defense of his countrymen, others siding with the immaculately dressed Todd, so correct in his every appointment that he was never known, during the whole voyage, to wear a pair of socks that did not in color and design match his cravat.

. . . .

The chief steward had given us seats at the end of one of the small tables. The Doctor sat under the porthole, and Todd and I had the chairs on either side of him. The two end seats — those on the aisle — were occupied by a girl of twenty-five, simply clad in a plain black dress with plainer linen collar and cuffs, and a young German. The girl would always arrive late, and would sink into her revolving chair with a languid movement, as if the voyage had told upon her. Often her face was pale and her eyes were heavy and red, as if from want of sleep. The young German — a Baron von Hoffbein, the passenger list said — was one of those self-possessed, good-natured, pink-cheeked young Teutons, with blue eyes, blond hair, and a tiny waxed mustache, a mere circumflex accent of a mustache, over his "o" of a mouth. His sponsors in baptism had doubtless sent him across the sea to chase the wild boar or the rude buffalo, with the ultimate design, perhaps, of founding a brewery in some Western city.

The manners of this young aristocrat toward the girl were an especial source of delight to Todd, who watched his every movement with the keenest interest. Whenever the baron approached the table he would hesitate a moment, as if in doubt as to which particular chair he should occupy, and, with an apologetic hand on his heart and a slight bow, drop into a seat immediately opposite hers. Then he would raise a long, thin arm aloft and snap his fingers to call a passing waiter. I noticed that he always ordered the same breakfast, beginning with cold sausage and ending with pancakes. During the repast the young girl opposite him would talk to him in a simple, straightforward way, quite as a sister would have done, and without the slightest trace of either coquetry or undue reserve.

When we were five days out, a third person occupied a seat at one side of the young woman. He was a man of perhaps sixty years of age, with big shoulders and big body, and a great round head covered with a mass of dull white hair which fell about his neck and forehead. The newcomer was dressed in a suit of gray cloth, much worn and badly cut, the coat collar, by reason of the misfit, being hunched up under his hair. This gave him the appearance of a man without a shirt collar, until a turn of his head revealed his clean starched linen and narrow black cravat. He looked like a plain, well-to-do manufacturer or contractor, one whose earlier years had been spent in the out of doors; for the weather had left its mark on his neck, where one can always look for signs of a man's manner of life. His was that of a man who had worn low-collared flannel shirts most of his days. He had, too, a look of determination, as if he had been accustomed to be obeyed. He was evidently an invalid, for his cheeks were sunken and pale, with the pallor that comes of long confinement.

Apart from these characteristics there was nothing specially remarkable about him except the two cavernous eye sockets, sunk in his head, the shaggy eyebrows arched above them, and the two eyes which blazed and flashed with the inward fire of black opals. As these rested first on one object and then on another, brightening or paling as he moved his head, I could not but think of the action of some alert searchlight gleaming out of a misty night.

As soon as he took his seat, the young woman, whose face for the first time since she had been on board had lost its look of anxiety and fatigue, leaned over him smilingly and began adjusting a napkin about his throat and pinning it to his coat. He smiled in response as she finished — a smile of singular sweetness — and held her hand until she regained her seat. They seemed as happy as children or as two lovers, laughing with each other, he now and then stopping to stroke her hand at some word which I could not hear. When, a moment after, the von Hoffbein took his accustomed seat, in full dress, too, — a red silk lining to his waistcoat, and a red silk handkerchief tucked in above it and worn liver-pad fashion, — the girl said simply, looking toward the man in gray, "My father, sir;" whereupon the young fellow shot up out of his chair, clicked his heels together, crooked his back, placed two fingers on his right eyebrow, and sat down again. The man in gray looked at him curiously and held out his hand, remarking that he was pleased to meet him.

Todd was also watching the group, for I heard him say to the Doctor: "These high-class Germans seldom forget themselves. The young baron saluted the old duffer with the bib as though he were his superior officer."

"Should n't wonder if he were," replied the Doctor, who had been looking intently over his soup spoon at the man in gray, and who was now summing up the circumflex accent, the red edges of the waistcoat, the liver-pad handkerchief, and the rest of von Hoffbein.

"You don't like him, evidently, my dear Doctor."

"You saw him first, Todd — you can have him. I prefer the old duffer, as you call him," answered the Doctor dryly, and put an end to the talk in that direction.

Soon the hum of voices filled the saloon,

rising above the clatter of the dishes and the occasional popping of corks. The baron and the man in gray had entered into conversation almost at once, and could be distinctly heard from where we sat, particularly the older man, who was doubtless unconscious of the carrying power of his voice. Such words as "working classes," "the people," "democracy," "when I was in Germany," etc., intermingling with the high-keyed tones of the baron's broken English, were noticeable above the din; the young girl listening smilingly, her eyes on those of her father. Then I saw the gray man bend forward, and heard him say with great earnestness, and in a voice that could be heard by the occupants of all the tables near our own: —

"It is a great thing to be an American, sir. I never realized it until I saw how things were managed on the other side. It must take all the ambition out of a man not to be able to do what he wants to do and what he knows he can do better than anybody else, simply because somebody higher than he says he shan't. We have our periods of unrest, and our workers sometimes lose their heads, but we always come out right in the end. There is no place in the world where a man has such opportunities as in my country. All he wants is brains and some little horse sense, — the country will do the rest."

Our end of the table had stopped to listen; so had the occupants of the tables on either side; so had Todd, who was patting the Doctor's arm, his face beaming.

"Listen to him, Doctor! Hear that voice! How like a traveling American! There 's one of your ex*trawd*'nary clay-soiled sons of toil out on an educating tour: are n't you proud of him? Oh, it 's too delicious!"

For once I agreed with Todd. The peculiar strident tones of the man in gray had jarred upon my nerves. I saw, too, that one lady, with slightly elevated shoulder, had turned her back and was addressing her neighbor.

The Doctor had not taken his eyes from the gray man, and had not lost a word of his talk. As Todd finished speaking, the daughter, with all tenderness and with a pleased glance into her father's eyes, arose, and putting her hand in his helped him to his feet, the baron standing at "attention." As the American started to leave the table, and his big shaggy head and broad shoulders reached their full height, the Doctor leaned forward, craning his head eagerly. Then he turned to Todd, and in his crisp, incisive way said: "Todd, the matter with you is that you never see any further than your nose. You ought to be ashamed of yourself. Look at his empty sleeve; off at the shoulder, too!"

II

IN the smoking-room that night a new and peculiar variety of passenger made his appearance, and his first one — to me — although we were then within two days of Sandy Hook. This individual wore a check suit of the latest London cut, big broad-soled Piccadilly shoes, and smoked a brierwood pipe which he constantly filled from a rubber pouch carried in his waistcoat pocket. When I first noticed him, he was sitting at a table with two Englishmen drinking brandy-and-sodas, — plural, not singular.

The Doctor, Todd, and I were at an adjoining table: the Doctor immersed in a scientific pamphlet, Todd sipping his crème de menthe, and I my coffee. Over in one corner were a group of drummers playing poker. They had not left the spot since we started, except at meal-time and at midnight, when Fritz, the smoking-room steward, had turned them out to air the room. Scattered about were other passengers—some reading, some playing checkers or backgammon, others asleep, among them the pink-cheeked von Hoffbein, who lay sprawled out on one of the leather-covered sofas, his thin legs spread apart like the letter A, as he emitted long-drawn organ tones, with only the nose stop pulled out.

The party of Englishmen, by reason of the unlimited number of brandy-and-sodas which their comrade in the check suit had ordered for them, were more or less noisy, laughing a good deal. They had attracted the attention of the whole room, many of the old-timers wondering how long it would be before the third officer would tap the check suit on the shoulder, and send it and him to bed under charge of a steward. The constant admonitions of his companions seemed to have had no effect upon the gentleman in question, for he suddenly launched out upon such topics as Colonial Policies and Governments and Taxation and Modern Fleets; addressing his remarks, not to his two friends, but to the room at large.

According to my own experience, the

traveling Englishman is a quiet, well-bred, reticent man, brandy-and-soda proof (I have seen him drink a dozen of an evening without a droop of an eyelid); and if he has any positive convictions of the superiority of that section of the Anglo-Saxon race to which he belongs, — and he invariably has, — he keeps them to himself, certainly in the public smoking-room of a steamer filled with men of a dozen different nations. The outbreak, as well as the effect of the incentive, was therefore as unexpected as it was unusual.

The check-suit man, however, was not constructed along these lines. The spirit of old Hennessy was in his veins, the stored energy of many sodas pressed against his tongue, and an explosion was inevitable. No portion of these excitants, strange to say, had leaked into his legs, for outwardly he was as steady as an undertaker. He began again, his voice pitched in a high key: —

"Talk of coercing England! Why, we 've got a hundred and forty-one ships of the line, within ten days' sail of New York, that could blow the bloody stuffin' out of every man Jack of 'em. And we don't care a brass farthing what Uncle Sam says about it, either."

His two friends tried to keep him quiet, but he broke out again on Colonization and American Treachery and Conquest of Cuba; and so, being desirous to read in peace, I nodded to the Doctor and Todd, picked up my book, and drew up a steamer chair on the deck outside, under one of the electric lights.

I had hardly settled myself in my seat when a great shout went up from the smoking-room that sent every one running down the deck, and jammed the portholes and doors of the room with curious faces. Then I heard a voice rise clear above the noise inside: "Not another word, sir; you don't know what you are talking about. We Americans don't rob people we give our lives to free."

I forced my way past the door, and stepped inside. The Englishman was being held down in his chair by his two friends. In his effort to break loose he had wormed himself out of his coat. Beside their table, close enough to put his hand on any one of them, stood the Doctor, a curious set expression on his face. Todd was outside the circle, standing on a sofa to get a better view.

Towering above the Englishman, his eyes

burning, his shaggy hair about his face, his whole figure tense with indignation, was the man with the empty sleeve! Close behind him, cool, polite, straight as a gendarme, and with the look in his eye of a cat about to spring, stood the young baron. As I reached the centre of the mêlée, wondering what had been the provocation and who had struck the first blow, I saw the baron lean forward, and heard him say in a low voice to one of the Englishmen, "He is so old as to be his fadder; take me," and he tapped his chest meaningly with his fingers. Evidently he had not fenced at Heidelberg for nothing, if he did have pink cheeks and pipestem legs.

The old man turned and laid his hand on the baron's shoulder. "I thank you, sir, but I'll attend to this young man." His voice had lost all its rasping quality now. It was low and concentrated, like that of one accustomed to command. "Take your hands off him, gentlemen, if you please. I don't think he has so far lost his senses as to strike a man twice his age and with one arm. Now, sir, you will apologize to me, and to the room, and to your own friends, who must be heartily ashamed of your conduct."

At the bottom of almost every Anglo-Saxon is a bed rock of common sense that you reach through the shifting sands of prejudice with the probe of fair play. The young man in the check suit, who was now on his feet, looked the speaker straight in the eye, and, half drunk as he was, held out his hand. "I'm sorry, sir, I offended you. I was speaking to my friends here, and I did not know any Americans were present."

"Bravo!" yelled the Doctor. "What did I tell you Todd? That's the kind of stuff! Now, gentlemen, all together—three cheers for the man with the empty sleeve!"

Everybody broke out with another shout—all but Todd, who had not made the slightest response to the Doctor's invitation to loosen his legs and his lungs. He did not show the slightest emotion over the fracas, and, moreover, seemed to have become suddenly disgusted with the baron.

Then the Doctor grasped the young German by the hand, and said how glad he was to know him, and how delighted he would be if he would join them and "take something,"—all of which the young man accepted with a frank, pleased look on his face.

When the room had resumed its normal

conditions, all three Englishmen having disappeared, the Doctor, whose enthusiasm over the incident had somehow paved the way for closer acquaintance, introduced me in the same informal way both to the baron and to the hero of the occasion, as "a brother American," and we all sat down beside the old man, his face lighting up with a smile as he made room for us. Then laying his hand on my knee, with the manner of an older man, he said: "I ought not to have given way, perhaps; but the truth is, I 'm not accustomed to hear such things at home. I did not know until I got close to him that he had been drinking, or I might have let it pass. I suppose this kind of talk may always go on in the smoking-room of these steamers. I don't know, for it 's my first trip abroad, and on the way out I was too ill to leave my berth. To-night is the first time I 've been in here. It was bad for me, I suppose. I 've been ill all" —

He stopped suddenly, caught his breath quickly, and his hand fell from my knee. For a moment he sat leaning forward, breathing heavily.

I sprang up, thinking he was about to faint. The baron started for a glass of water. The old man raised his hand.

"No, don't be alarmed, gentlemen; it is nothing. I am subject to these attacks; it will pass off in a moment," and he glanced around the room as if to assure himself that no one but ourselves had noticed it.

"The excitement was too much for you," the Doctor said gravely, in an undertone. His trained eye had caught the peculiar pallor of the face. "You must not excite yourself so."

"Yes, I know, — the heart," he said after a pause, speaking with short, indrawn breaths, and straightening himself slowly and painfully until he had regained his old erect position. After a little while he put his hand again on my knee, with an added graciousness in his manner, as if in apology for the shock he had given me. "It 's passing off, — yes, I 'm better now." Then, in a more cheerful tone, as if to change the subject, he added: "My steward tells me that we made four hundred and fifty-two miles yesterday. This makes my little girl happy. She 's had an anxious summer, and I 'm glad this part of it is over. Yes, she 's *very* happy to-day."

"You mean on account of your health?" I asked sympathetically; although I remembered afterward that I had not caught his meaning.

"Well, not so much that, for that can never be any better, but on account of our being so near home, — only two days more. I could n't bear to leave her alone on shipboard, but it 's all right now. You see, there are only two of us since her mother died." His voice fell, and for the first time I saw a shade of sadness cross his face. The Doctor saw it too, for there was a slight quaver in his voice when he said, as he rose, that his stateroom was No. 13, and he would be happy to be called upon at any time, day or night, whenever he could be of service; then he resumed his former seat under the light, and apparently his pamphlet, although I could see his eyes were constantly fixed on the pallid face.

The baron and I kept our seats, and I ordered three of something from Fritz, as further excuse for tarrying beside the invalid. I wanted to know something more of a man who was willing to fight the universe with one arm in defense of his country's good name, though I was still in the dark as to what had been the provocation. All I could gather from the young baron, in his broken English, was that the Englishman had maligned the motives of our government in helping the Cubans, and that the old man had flamed out, astounding the room with the power of his invective and thorough mastery of the subject, and compelling their admiration by the genuineness of his outburst.

"I see you have lost your arm," I began, hoping to get some further facts regarding himself.

"Yes, some years ago," he answered simply, but with a tone that implied he did not care to discuss either the cause or the incidents connected with its loss.

"An accident?" I asked. The empty sleeve seemed suddenly to have a peculiar fascination for me.

"Yes, partly," and, smiling gravely, he rose from his seat, saying that he must rejoin his daughter, who might be worrying. He bade the occupants of the room good-night, many of whom, including the baron and the Doctor, rose to their feet, — the baron saluting, and following the old man out, as if he had been his superior officer.

With the closing of the smoking-room door, P. Wooverman Shaw Todd, Esquire, roused himself from his chair, walked toward the Doctor, and sat down beside him.

"Well! I must say that I'm glad that man's gone!" he burst out. "I have never seen anything more outrageous than this whole performance. This fire eater ought to travel about with a guardian. Suppose, now, my dear Doctor, that everybody went about with these absurd ideas, — what a place the world would be to live in! This is the worst American I have met yet. And see what an example; even the young baron lost his head, I am sorry to say. I heard the young Englishman's remark. It was, I admit, indiscreet, but no part of it was addressed to this very peculiar person; and it is just like that kind of an American, full of bombast and bluster, to feel offended. Besides, every word the young man said was true. There is a great deal of politics in this Cuban business, — you know it, and I know it. We have no men trained for colonial life, and we never shall have, so long as our better clarss keep aloof from politics. The island will bc made a camping-ground for vulgar politicians — no question about it. Think, now, of sending that firebrand among those people. You can see by his very appearance that he has never done anything better than astonish the loungers about a country stove. As for all this fuss about his empty sleeve, no doubt some other fire eater put a bullet through it in defense of what such kind of people call their honor. It is too farcical for words, my dear Doctor, — too farcical for words," and P. Wooverman Shaw Todd, Esquire, pulled his steamer cap over his eyes, jumped to his feet, and stalked out of the room.

The Doctor looked after Todd until he had disappeared. Then he turned to his pamphlet again. There was evidently no composite, explosive epithet deadly enough within reach at the moment, or there is not the slightest doubt in my mind that he would have demolished Todd with it.

Todd's departure made another vacancy at our table, and a tall man, who had applauded the loudest at the apology of the Englishman, dropped into Todd's empty chair, addressing the Doctor as representing our party.

"I suppose you know who the old man is, don't you?"

"No."

"That 's John Stedman, manager of the Union Iron Works of Parkinton, a manufacturing town in my State. He 's one of the best iron men in the country. Fine old fellow, is n't he? He 's been ill ever since his wife died, and I don't think he 'll ever get over it. She had been sick for years, and he nursed her day and night. He would n't go to Congress, preferring to stay by her, and it almost broke his heart when she died. Poor old man, — don't look as if he was long for this world. I expected him to mop up the floor with that Englishman, sick as he is; and he would, if he had n't apologized. I heard, too, what your friend who has just gone out said about Stedman not being the kind of a man to send to Cuba. I tell you, they might look the country over, and they could n't find a better. That 's been his strong hold, straightening out troubles of one kind or another. Everybody believes in him, and anybody takes his word. He 's done a power of good in our State."

"In what way?" asked the Doctor.

"Oh, in settling strikes, for one thing. You see, he started from the scrap pile, and he knows the laboring man down to a dot, for he carried a dinner pail himself for ten years of his life. When the men are imposed upon he stands by 'em, and compels the manufacturers to deal square; and if they don't, he joins the men and fights it out with the bosses. If the men are wrong, and want what the furnaces can't give 'em, — and there 's been a good deal of that lately, — he sails into the gangs, and, if nothing else will do, he gets a gun and joins the sheriffs. He was all through that last strike we had, three years ago, and it would be going on now but for John Stedman."

"But he seems to be a man of fine education," interrupted the Doctor, who was listening attentively.

"Yes, so he is,—learned it all at night schools. When he was a boy he used to fire the kilns, and they say you could always find him with a spelling-book in one hand and a chunk of wood in the other, reading nights by the light of the kiln fires."

"You say he went to Congress?" The Doctor's eyes were now fixed on the speaker.

"No, I said he *would* n't go. His wife was taken sick about that time, and when he found she was n't going to get well,—she had lung trouble,—he told the committee that he would n't accept the nomination; and of course nomination meant election for him. He told 'em his wife had stuck by him all her life, had washed his flannel shirts for him and cooked his dinner, and that he was going to stick by her now she was down. But I tell you what he did do: he stumped the district for his opponent, because he said he was a better man than his own party put up,—and elected him, too. That was just like

John Stedman. The heelers were pretty savage, but that made no difference to him.

"He 's never recovered from his wife's death. That daughter with him is the only child he 's got. She 's been so afraid he 'd die on board and have to be buried at sea that he 's kept his berth just to please her. The doctor at home told him Carlsbad was his only chance, and the daughter begged so he made the trip. He was so sick when he went out that he took a coffin with him, — it 's in the hold now. I heard him tell his daughter this morning that it was all right now, and he thought he 'd get up. You see, there are only two days more, and the captain promised the daughter not to bury her father at sea when we were that close to land. Stedman smiled when he told me, but that 's just like him ; he 's always been cool as a cucumber."

"How did he lose his arm ?" I inquired. I had been strangely absorbed in what he had told me. "In the war ?"

"No. He served two years, but that 's not how he lost his arm. He lost it saving the lives of some of his men. I happened to be up at Parkinton at the time, buying some coke, and I saw him carried out. It was about ten years ago. He had invented a new furnace; 'most all the new wrinkles they 've got at the Union Company Stedman made for 'em. When they got ready to draw the charge, — that 's when the red-hot iron is about to flow out of the furnace, you know, the outlet got clogged. That 's a bad thing to happen to a furnace; for if a chill should set in, the whole plant would be ruined. Then, again, it might explode and tear everything to pieces. Some of the men jumped into the pit with their crowbars, and began to jab away at the opening in the wrong place, and the metal started with a rush. Stedman hollered to 'em to stop; but they either did n't hear him or would n't mind. Then he jumped in among them, threw them out of the way, grabbed a crowbar, and fought the flow until they all got out safe. But the hot metal had about cooked his arm clear to the elbow before he let go."

The Doctor, with hands deep in his pockets, began pacing the floor. Then he stopped, and, looking down at me, said slowly, pointing off his fingers one after the other to keep count as he talked: —

"Tender and loyal to his wife — thoughtful of his child — facing death like a hero — a soldier and patriot. What is there in the make-up of a gentleman that this man has n't got?

"Come! Let 's go out and find that high-collared, silk-stockinged, sweet-scented Anglomaniac from Salem! By the Eternal, Todd 's got to apologize!"

"TINCTER OV IRON"

IT was in an old town in Connecticut. Marbles kept the shop. "Joseph Marbles, Shipwright and Blacksmith," the sign read.

I knew Joe. He had repaired one of the lighters used in carrying materials for the foundation of the lighthouse I was building. The town lay in the barren end of the State, where they raised rocks enough to make four stone fences to the acre. Joe always looked to me as if he had lived off the crop. The diet never affected his temper nor hardened his heart, so far as I could see. It was his body, his long, lean, lank body, that suggested the stone diet.

In his early days Joe had married a helpmate. She had lasted until the beginning of the third year, and then she had been carried to the cemetery on the hill, and another stone, and a new one, added to the general assortment. This matrimonial episode was his last.

This wife was a constant topic with Marbles. He would never speak of her as a part of his life, one who had shared his bed and board, and therefore entitled to his love and reverent remembrance. It was rather as an appendage to his household, a curiosity, a natural freak, as one would discuss the habits of a chimpanzee, and with a certain pity, too, for the poor creature whom he had housed, fed, poked at, humored, and then buried.

And yet with it all I could always see that nothing else in his life had made so profound an impression upon him as the companionship of this "poor creeter," and that underneath his sparsely covered ribs there still glowed a spot for the woman who had given him her youth.

He would say, "It wuz one ov them days when she would n't eat, or it was kind o' cur'us to watch her go on when she had one ov them tantrums." Sometimes he would recount some joke he had played upon her, rubbing his ribs in glee—holding his sides would have been a superfluous act and the statement here erroneous.

"That wuz when she fust come, yer know," he said to me one day, leaning against an old boat, his adze in his hand. "Her folks belonged over to Westerly. I never had seen much ov wimmen, and did n't know their ways. But I tell yer she wuz a queer 'un, allers imaginin' she wuz ailin', er had heart disease when she got out er breath runnin' upstairs, er as'mer, er lumbago, er some-thin' else dreadful. She wuz the cur'usest critter too to take medicin' ye ever see. She never ailed none really 'cept when she broke her coller bone a-fallin' downstairs, and in the last sickness, the one that killed her, but she believed all the time she wuz, which was wuss. Every time the druggist would git out a new red card and stick it in his winder, with a cure fer cold, or chil-blains, er croup, er e'sipelas, she 'd go and buy it, an' out 'd cum ther cork, and she a-tastin' ov it 'fore she got hum. She used ter rub herself with St. Jiminy's intment, and soak her feet in sea-salt, and cover herself with plasters till yer could n't rest. Why, ther cum a feller once who painted a yaller sign on ther whole side ov Buck-ley's barn — cure fer spiral meningeetius, — and she wuz nigh crazy till she had found out where ther pain ought ter be, and had clapped er plaster on her back and front, persuadin' herself she had it. That 's how she bruk her coller bone, a-runnin' fer hot water to soak 'em off, they burnt so, and stumblin' over a kit ov tools I had brung hum to do a job around the house. After this she begun ter run down so, and git so thin and peaked, I begun to think she really wuz goin' ter be sick, after all, jest fer a change.

" When ther doctor come he sed it warn't nothin' but druggist's truck that ailed her, and he throwed what there wuz out er ther winder, and give her a tonic — Tincter ov Iron he called it. Well, yer never see a woman hug a thing as she did that bottle. It was a spoonful three times a day, and then she 'd reach out fer it in ther night, vowin' it was doin' her a heap er good, and I a-gettin' ther bottle filled at Sarcy's ther druggist's, and payin' fifty cents every time he put er new cork in it. I tried ter reason with her, but it warn't no use; she would have it, and if she could have got outer bed and looked round at the spring crop of advertisements on ther fences, she would hev struck somethin' worse. So I let her run on until she tuk about seven dollars' wuth of Tincter, and then I dropped in ter Sarcy's. 'Sarcy,' sez I, 'can't ye wholesale this, er sell it by the quart? If the ole woman's coller bone don't get ter runnin' easy purty soon I 'll be broke.'

" 'Well,' he said, 'if I bought a dozen it might come cheaper, but it wuz a mighty perticler medicine, and had ter be fixed jest so.'

" ''Taint pizen, is it?' I sez, 'thet 's got ter

be fixed so all-fired kerful?' He 'lowed it warn't, and thet ye might take er barrel of it and it would n't kill yer, but all ther same it has ter be made mighty pertic'ler.

"'Well, iron 's cheap enough,' I sez, 'and strengthenin', too. If it 's ther Tincter thet costs so, don't put so much in.' Well, he laffed, and said ther warn't no real iron in it, only Tincter, kinder iron soakage like, same es er drawin' ov tea.

" Goin' home thet night I got ter thinkin'. I 'd been round iron all my life and knowed its ways, but I had n't struck no Tincter as I knowed ov. When she fell asleep I poured out a leetle in another bottle and slid it in my trousers pocket, an' next day, down ter ther shop, I tasted ov it and held it up ter ther light. It was kind er persimmony and dark-lookin', ez if it had rusty nails in it; and so thet night when I goes hum I sez ter her, 'Down ter ther other druggist's I kin git twice as much Tincter fer fifty cents as I kin at Sarcy's, and if yer don't mind I 'll git it filled there.' Well, she never kicked a stroke, 'cept to say I 'd better hurry, fer she had n't had a spoonful sence daylight, and she wuz beginnin' ter feel faint. When the whistle blew I cum hum ter dinner, and sot the new bottle, about twice as big as the other one, beside her bed.

"'How's that?' I sez. 'It's a leetle grain darker and more muddy like, but the new druggist sez thet's the Tincter, and thet's what's doin' ov yer good.' Well, she never suspicioned; jest kept on, night and day, wrappin' herself round it every two er three hours, I gettin' it filled regerlar and she a-empt'in' ov it.

"'Bout four weeks arter that she begun to git around, and then she'd walk out ez fur ez ther shipyard fence, and then, begosh, she begun to flesh up so as you would n't know her. Now an' then she'd meet the doctor, and she'd say how she'd never a-lived but fer ther Tincter, and he'd laff and drive on. When she got real peart I brought her down to the shop one day, and I shows her an old paint keg thet I kep' rusty bolts in, and half full ov water.

"'Smell that,' I sez, and she smells it and cocks her eye.

"'Taste it,' I sez, and she tasted it, and give me a look. Then I dips a spoonful out in a glass, and I sez: 'It's most time to take yer medicine. I kin beat Gus Sarcy all holler makin' Tincter; every drop yer drunk fer a month come out er thet keg.'"

"FIVE MEALS FOR A DOLLAR"

THE Literary Society of West Norrington, Vt., had invited me to lecture on a certain Tuesday night in February.

The Tuesday night had arrived. So had the train. So had the knock-kneed, bandy-legged hack — two front wheels bowed in, two hind wheels bowed out — and so had the lecturer.

West Norrington is built on a hill. At the foot are the station, a saw-mill, and a glue factory. On the top is a flat plateau holding the principal residences, printing-office, opera-house, confectionery store, druggist's, and hotel. Up the incline is a scattering of cigar-stores, butcher shops, real-estate agencies, and one lone restaurant. You know it is a restaurant by the pile of extra-dry oyster-shells in the window — oysterless for months — and the four oranges bunched together in a wire basket like a nest of pool balls. You know it also from the sign —

"Five meals for a dollar."

I saw this sign on my way up the hill, but it made no impression on my mind. I was bound for the hotel — the West Norrington Arms, the conductor called it; and as I had eaten nothing since seven o'clock, and it was then four, I was absorbed mentally in arranging a bill of fare. Broiled chicken, of course, I said to myself — always get delicious broiled chicken in the country — and a salad, and perhaps — you can't always tell, of course, what the cellars of these old New England taverns may contain — yes, perhaps a pint of any really good Burgundy, Pommard, or Beaune.

"West Norrington Arms" sounded well. There was a distinct flavor of exclusiveness and comfort about it, suggesting old side-boards, hand-polished tables, small bar with cut-glass decanters, Franklin stoves in the bedrooms, and the like. I could already see the luncheon served in my room, the bright wood fire lighting up the dimity curtains draping the high-post bedstead. Yes, I would order Pommard.

Here the front knees came together with a jerk. Then the driver pulled his legs out of a buffalo-robe, opened the door with a twist, and called out, —

"Nor'n't'n Arms."

I got out.

The first glance was not reassuring. It was perhaps more Greek than Colonial or Early English or Late Dutch. Four high wooden boxes, painted brown, were set up on end — Doric columns these — supporting a pediment of like material and color. Half-way up these supports hung a balcony, where the Fourth of July orator always stands when he addresses his fellow citizens. Old, of course, I said to myself — early part of this century. Not exactly moss-covered and inn-like, as I expected to find, but inside it 's all right.

"Please take in that bag and fur overcoat." This to the driver, in a cheery tone.

The clerk was leaning over the counter, chewing a toothpick. Evidently he took me for a drummer, for he stowed the bag behind the desk, and hung the overcoat up on a nail in a side room opening out of the office, and within reach of his eye.

When I registered my name it made no perceptible change in his manner. He said, "Want supper?" with a tone in his voice that convinced me he had not heard a word of the Event which brought me to West Norrington — I being the Event.

"No, not now. I would like you to send to my room in half an hour a broiled chicken, some celery, and any vegetable which you can get ready — and be good enough to put a pint of Burgundy" —

I did n't get any further. Something in his manner attracted me. I had not looked at him with any degree of interest before. He had been merely a medium for trunk check, room key, and ice water — nothing more.

Now I did. I saw a young man — a mean-looking young man — with a narrow, squeezed face, two flat glass eyes sewed in with red cotton, and a disastrous complexion. His hair was brushed like a barber's, with a scooping curl over the forehead; his neck was long and thin — so long that his apple looked over his collar's edge. This collar ran down to a white shirt decorated with a gold pin, the whole terminating in a low-cut velvet vest.

"Supper at seven," he said.

This, too, came with a jerk.

"Yes, I know, but I have n't eaten anything since breakfast, and don't want to wait until" —

"Ain't nuthin' cooked 'tween meals. Supper at seven."

"Can't I get" —

"Yer can't get nuthin' until supper-time, and yer won't get no Burgundy then. Yer could n't get a bottle in Norrington with a club. This town 's prohibition. Want a room?" This last word was almost shouted in my ear.

"Yes — one with a wood fire." I kept my temper.

"Front!" — this to a boy half asleep on a bench. "Take this bag to No. 37, and turn on the steam. Your turn next" — and he handed the pen to a fresh arrival, who had walked up from the train.

No. 37 contained a full set of Michigan furniture, including a patent wash-stand that folded up to look like a bookcase, smelt slightly of varnish, and was as hot as a Pullman sleeper.

I threw up all the windows; came down and tackled the clerk again.

"Is there a restaurant near by?"

"Next block above. Nichols."

He never looked up — just kept on chewing the toothpick.

"Is there another hotel here?"

Even a worm will turn.

"No."

That settled it. I did n't know any inhabitant — not even a committeeman. It was the West Norrington Arms or the street.

So I started for Nichols. By that time I could have eaten the shingles off the church.

Nichols proved to be a one-and-a-half-story house with a glass door, a calico curtain, and a jingle bell. Inside was a cake shop, presided over by a thin woman in a gingham dress and black lace cap and wig. In the rear stood a marble-top table with iron legs. This made it a restaurant.

"*Five Meals for a Dollar*"

"Can you get me something to eat? Steak, ham and eggs — anything?" I had fallen in my desires.

She looked me all over. "Well, I 'm 'mazin' sorry, but I guess you 'll have to excuse us; we 're just bakin', and this is our busy day. S'mother time we should like to, but to-day" —

I closed the door and was in the street again. I had no time for lengthy discussions that did n't lead to something tangible and eatable.

"Alone in London," I said to myself. "Lost in New York. Adrift in West Norrington. Plenty of money to buy, and nobody to sell. Everybody going about their business with full stomachs, happy, contented, — all with homes, and firesides, and ice chests, and things hanging to cellar rafters, hams and such like, and I a wanderer and hungry, an outcast, a tramp."

Then I thought some citizen might take

me in. She was a rather amiable-looking old lady, with a kind, motherly face.

"Madam!" This time I took off my hat. Ah, the common law of hunger brings you down and humbles your pride. "Do you live here, madam?"

"Why, yes, sir," edging to the sidewalk.

"Madam, I am a stranger here, and very hungry. It 's baking-day at Nichols. Do you know where I can get anything to eat?"

"Well, no, I can't rightly say," still eyeing me suspiciously. "Hungry, be ye? Well, that 's too bad, and Nichols baking."

I corroborated all these statements, standing bare-headed, a wild idea running through my head that her heart would soften and she would take me home and set me down in a big chintz-covered rocking chair, near the geraniums in the windows, and have her daughter — a nice, fresh, rosy-cheeked girl in an apron — go out into the buttery and bring in white cheese, and big slices of bread, and some milk, and preserves, and a — But the picture was never completed.

"Well," she said slowly, "if Nichols is baking, I guess ye 'll hev to wait till supper-time."

Then like a sail to a drowning man there

rose before me the sign down the hill near the station, "Five meals for a dollar."

"Five Meals for a Dollar"

I had the money. I had the appetite. I would eat them all at once, and *now*.

In five minutes I was abreast of the extra-dry oyster-shells and the pool balls. Then I pushed open the door.

Inside there was a long room, bare of everything but a wooden counter, upon which stood a glass case filled with cigars; behind this was a row of shelves with jars of candy, and level with the lower shelf my eye caught a slouch hat. The hat covered the head of the proprietor. He was sitting on a stool, sorting out chewing-gum.

"Can I get something to eat?"

The hat rose until it stood six feet in the air, surmounting a round, good-natured face, ending in a chin whisker.

"Cert. What'll yer hev?"

Here at last was peace and comfort and food and things! I could hardly restrain myself.

"Anything. Steak, fried potatoes — what have you got?"

"Waal, I dunno. 'Tain't time yit for supper, but we kin fix ye somehow. Lemme see."

Then he pushed back a curtain that

screened one half of the room, disclosing three square tables with white cloths and casters, and disappeared through a rear door.

"We got a steak," he said, dividing the curtains again, "but the potatoes is out."

"Any celery?"

"No. Guess can git ye some 'cross to ther grocery. Won't take a minit."

"All right. Could you" — and I lowered my voice — "could you get me a bottle of beer?"

"Yes — if you got a doctor's prescription."

"Could *you* write one?" I asked nervously.

"I 'll try." And he laughed.

In two minutes he was back, carrying four bunches of celery and a paper box marked "Paraffine candles."

"What preserves have you?"

"Waal, any kind."

"Raspberry jam, or apricots?" I inquired, my spirits rising.

"We ain't got no rusberry, but we got peaches."

"Anything else?"

"Waal, no; come ter look 'em over, just peaches."

So he added a can to the celery and candles, and carried the whole to the rear.

While he was gone I leaned over the cigar-case and examined the stock. One box labeled "Bouquet" attracted my eye; each cigar had a little paper band around its middle. I remembered the name, and determined to smoke one after dinner if it took my last cent.

Then a third person took a hand in the feast. This was the hired girl, who came in with a tray. She wore an alpaca dress and a disgusted expression. It was evident that she resented my hunger as a personal affront — stopping everything to get supper two hours ahead of time! She did n't say this aloud, but I knew it all the same.

Then more tray, with a covered dish the size of a soap-cup, a few sprigs of celery out of the four bunches, and a preserve-dish, about the size of a butter pat, containing four pieces of peach swimming in their own juice.

In the soap-dish lay the steak. It was four inches in diameter and a quarter of an inch thick. I opened the paraffine candles, poured out half a glass, and demolished the celery and peaches. I did n't want to muss up the steak. I was afraid I might bend it, and spoil it for some one else.

Then an idea struck me: "Could she poach me some eggs?"

She supposed she could, if she could find the eggs; most everything was locked up this time of day.

I waited, and spread the mustard on the dry bread, and had more peaches and paraffine. When the eggs came they excited my sympathies. They were such innocent-looking things — pinched and shriveled up, as if they had fainted at sight of the hot water and died in great agony. The toast, too, on which they were coffined, had a cremated look. Even the hired girl saw this. She said it was a "leetle mite too much browned; she 'd forgot it watchin' the eggs."

Here the street door opened, and a young woman entered and asked for two papers of chewing-gum.

She got them, but not until the proprietor had shot together the curtains screening off the candy store from the restaurant. The dignity and exclusiveness of the establishment required this.

When she was gone I poured out the rest of the paraffine, and called out through the closed curtains for a cigar.

"One of them bo-kets?" came the proprietor's voice in response.

"Yes, one of them."

He brought it himself, in his hand, just as

"FORTY-TWO CENTS"

it was, holding the mouth end between the thumb and forefinger.

"And now how much?"

He made a rapid accounting, overlooking the table, his eyes lighting on the several fragments: "Beer, ten cents; steak, ten; peaches, five; celery, three; eggs on toast, ten; one bo-ket, four." Then he paused a moment, as if he wanted to be entirely fair and square, and said, "Forty-two cents."

When I reached the hotel, a man who said he was the proprietor came to my room. He was a sad man with tears in his voice.

"You 're comin' to supper, ain't ye? It 'll be the last time. It 's a kind o' mournful occasion, but I like to have ye."

It was now my turn.

"No, I 'm not coming to supper. You drove me out of here half starving into the street two hours ago. I could n't get anything to eat at Nichols, and so I had to go down the hill to a place near the saw-mill, where I got the most infernal" —

He stopped me with a look of real anxiety.

"Not the five-meals-for-a-dollar place?"

"Yes."

"And you swallowed it?"

"Certainly — poached eggs, peaches, and a lot of things."

"No," he said reflectively, looking at me curiously. "*You* don't want no supper — prob'bility is you won't want no breakfast, either. You 'd better eaten the saw-mill — it would 'er set lighter. If I 'd known who you were I 'd tried" —

"But I told the clerk," I broke in.

"What clerk?" he interrupted in an astonished tone.

"Why, the clerk at the desk, where I registered — that long-necked crane with red eyes."

"He ain't no clerk; we ain't had one for a week. Don't you know what 's goin' on? Ain't you read the bills? Step out into the hall — there 's one posted up right in front of you. 'Sheriff's sale; all the stock and fixtures of the Norrington Arms to be sold on Wednesday morning' — that 's to-morrow — 'by order of the Court.' You can read the rest yourself; print 's too fine for me. That fellow you call a crane is a deputy sheriff. He 's takin' charge, while we eat up what 's in the house."

www.ingramcontent.com/pod-product-compliance
Lightning Source LLC
Chambersburg PA
CBHW020114030726
47498CB00006B/2106
9783743367029